# A is for Arrangement

## EDEN ADAMS

## FREE YOUR FANTASY
### Spicy Romance Series
### Book 1

# A racy rendezvous with a bold billionaire

Amber Lee is floored when she finds herself in a situation where she must make a special arrangement for her boss. She interviews woman after woman, but none is suitable - at least in her eyes.

Before he heads off to Dubai, Jordan needs a wife. What better arrangement than to volunteer herself?

# CHAPTER ONE

Amber's breath caught in her throat as she stared, wide-eyed, at her boss. "I'm sorry?" Her words came out in a breathless rush. Had she heard right? She frowned. "Did you say wife?"

Jordan leaned back in his chair, his lips curling in a sardonic smile. "That's exactly what I said. I leave for Dubai in two weeks, and when I do I must have a wife with me. Your job is to help me find one."

"I...I..." She drew in a shaky breath then swallowed. When she'd taken this job as executive assistant to Jordan Masters, owner and CEO of Masters Metals, never in a thousand years would she have imagined that one of her assignments would be the task of finding him a wife. As she stared at him, she clenched her hands tightly in her lap. "Where would I start?"

He shrugged. "Put an ad in the paper. Use social media. You have contacts on Facebook and Linkedin, don't you? The important thing is to screen the applicants, select high quality women, interview them, then choose the one you think would be the best for me." He inclined his head. "You can do this, Amber. I trust your judgment."

She suppressed a grimace. It sounded like Jordan Masters had a lot more confidence in her judgment than she did. How in the world do you choose a wife for one of the most discriminating men in the world? And why did he need one in such a rush, anyway?

"May I ask a question?" she dared venture. "Why do you need a wife for your trip to Dubai? I thought it was supposed to be a business trip."

"It is." Jordan expelled his breath in a snort. "I got myself into this mess. You're familiar with Sheikh Khalil Ali?"

"Yes, I've sent him correspondence on your behalf."

"He's a good friend of the family. Almost like an uncle to me." He heaved a sigh. "He's been harassing me about settling down, starting a family. Last time I got sick of it and told him I had someone in my life. Of course, he assumed I meant a wife. Now that I'm going to be in Dubai he wants me to bring her along. I'm supposed to introduce her to him."

Amber was still confused. "But isn't it easier to just admit that you made it all up? Why make things worse?"

He sighed again and this time he sat forward and propped his elbows on the desk. "You don't understand," he said, slowly shaking his head. "It's not as easy as that. It's better for me to take someone with me now and then later, a long time later, tell him that sadly we had to part."

She frowned. "You would go through all that?"

"To preserve Am Khalil's opinion of me, I would. It's that important to me and to the family." His gaze turned serious. "Listen. This is a big deal. Just trust me on that. I need you to get me a classy woman who can represent me well." He paused, a frown settling on his forehead. "And one who will follow orders. Having a pretend wife in the Middle East is one thing. Having a pretend wife who comes across as recalcitrant is a whole other story."

Amber bit her lip, his words swirling around in her head. Jordan needed a wife, a classy woman but a docile one, and all within the space of two weeks.

That was going to be a difficult task. But finding a suitable woman would not be the hard part. What would make the job difficult was the fact that she didn't want to find Jordan a wife at all. Of course, she wouldn't tell him that.

Amber cleared her throat. "Leave it to me," she said, as she pressed her notepad to her chest and got up. "I will get you the right woman for the job."

Her heart clenching as the words left her lips, she turned to go, but not before stealing a glance Jordan's way. The intensity of his stare almost made her pause. Had he read her mind somehow? Had she inadvertently given her reluctance away?

Quickly, she dropped her gaze and turned toward the door, eager to escape his questioning eyes. The last thing she needed was for her boss to notice any hint of resistance on her part.

Back in her office, safe from his stare, Amber slumped back in her seat, her gaze falling on the metal statuette that stood in the corner. As if it could sympathize with her dilemma, she gave it a wry smile. "So what would you do, Venus, Goddess of Love?" she asked. "After a year of working for this man, now he wants me to find him a wife. A wife..." Her voice trailed off as she turned her head to gaze out the window at the palm trees swaying in the wind. "Just when I thought he was beginning to notice me..." The softly whispered words ended in a hiccup.

The sad fact was, Amber Lee was in love with her boss, and had been since the day she walked through the doors of Masters Metals. She'd applied through Apple Employment Agency, and after going through the rigorous interview process she'd been selected from a group of nineteen applicants, all women, all eager to be working for one of the most respected businessmen in all of California, but also one of the youngest CEOs of a billion dollar enterprise. And it hadn't hurt that he was single.

That hadn't been Amber's primary reason for applying, though. Working for a handsome, sought-after billionaire bachelor was a definite perk, but what had attracted her to the position was the scope of the job, ranging from management to public relations to operations. In working so closely with the CEO, the lucky candidate would be exposed to critical aspects of business that would equip her to make a significant contribution to any corporation. Already six months into her MBA, Amber knew that such experience would be invaluable as she set her sights on a management position, and so she'd jumped at the chance.

And then she met Jordan Masters. Well over six feet tall, his presence dominated any room he entered. His straight-backed, solid physique didn't hurt, either. It was obvious that he was in perfect shape. But it was his striking features that were Amber's downfall - jet black, glossy hair framing a regal forehead, and a square jaw that spoke of strength and firmness of character, an aquiline nose leading to lips that promised pure passion. And then there were the eyes - deep, dark, intense pools that drew you in and never let you go. From the first time those eyes locked with hers, Jordan Masters had her body tingling all over.

She'd heard of sexual awareness but never had she felt it until the day she met her boss.

And then, to her dismay, the attraction grew until it had become a major source of distraction. Around Jordan her pulse would quicken, her breathing growing shallow, her mouth going dry. Thank goodness he'd never noticed any of it. At least, she didn't think he had.

But now, against the hidden desire of her heart, she would have to find him a woman. And soon.

It took three days of brooding before Amber finally worked up the courage to place the ad. "Businessman in need of professional pretend partner," it read. "Must possess superior acting abilities." It was the strangest social media post she'd ever made but she did it, providing an email address she'd set up specifically for the task.

As expected, the responses came flying in, fast and furious, email after email until, two days in, she had to close the door to any further applications. Then it was another two days of sifting and sorting until she whittled the pile down to a dozen. They'd posted photos, they'd attached resumes and one of them had even sent a video clip. And they were all beautiful, way too beautiful for Amber's liking.

"How's it going?" Jordan had asked, as he popped his head into her office on the third day of her search.

"Very well," she'd huffed, not letting on that she hadn't yet done a single interview.

"Do you think we'll be able to wrap this up by the end of the week?" he asked. "Before you know it, it will be time to leave for Dubai. I want to at least get to know the lady before it's time to go."

"Yes." Her grip tightened on the sheet of paper in her hand. "Just give me until the end of the week. I'll have the perfect girl for you."

When he left, closing the door behind him, she released her pent-up breath. She would select her top three applicants and interview them then pick the best candidate. There was no getting around it. Jordan was expecting an answer, in flesh and blood, by the end of the week.

The interviews were a challenge. "Sarah Smiley, how are you?" she greeted the first one. "Please come in."

Sarah was a petite brunette who seemed like she'd never had a bad day in her life. True to her name, she was smiling so broadly that Amber felt like she had to frown just to balance things out.

"Do you understand the nature of the job?" she asked the girl.

"I sure do," Little Miss Smiley gushed. "Mr. Masters is looking for the perfect wife and I'm the one."

"You are aware that this is an acting job, that Mr. Masters is looking for someone who can pretend to be his wife?"

"Pretend? He's not really looking for a wife?" The little brunette seemed genuinely confused. For the first time since she'd walked into the office her smile faltered.

Amber's gaze narrowed. Could the woman be so slow? "This is an acting job, Miss Smiley, a temporary role. Mr. Masters is not looking to get married."

"Oh." The woman's face fell. Clearly, she'd thought she would soon be walking down the aisle. Did she really think Jordan Masters was so lacking in interested women? If so, Miss Smiley really was slow.

"This is a business proposition, not a marriage proposal." Maybe Amber's tone was a bit more caustic than necessary but she was beginning to lose patience with the woman. What was worse - and this was a bit unfair to her visitor - the mention of the word marriage had annoyed the heck out of her. She couldn't even bear to think about Jordan, marriage and another woman, all in the same picture. No way. He was hers...at least in her mind.

She spent another few minutes grilling the now not-so-smiley applicant just so it didn't seem she wasn't giving her a fair chance, and then she sent her on her way. Any woman who could not understand an announcement for what it was - a job - was just a waste of time.

Amber's two other shortlisted applicants were not much better than the first. When Miss Tavish walked through the door she knew immediately that it wouldn't work. The woman oozed a confidence that was too haughty for her liking. Her nose in the air, she carried herself like the rest of the world was beneath her.

"Recent acting experience?" Amber asked as she fixed a cold stare on the woman, hoping to rattle her.

It didn't work. Clearly, Tanya Tavish was too self-assured to be intimidated by a mere executive assistant. "Of course. As you can see from my resume, I've had roles in some hit TV shows."

Amber glanced at the resume then raised her eyebrows. "Lion's Den, Miami Heat. Impressive. What parts did you play?"

"I...well...I was part of the crowd in the fight scene in episode three of Lion's Den, and I was a passerby in Miami Heat. The spots provided me with considerable acting experience."

"I see." Amber didn't bother to point out that any old Joe could have played those roles. She decided to change the subject. "And do you understand the scope of this job?"

"Of course." Tanya straightened up in her chair, looking like she was back to her old super-confident self. "Mr. Masters needs someone who can play the part of his wife. He's playing some sort of trick on his friends, I assume. I'll be happy to play the part. I plan on being the perfect wife. If I'm lucky, he'll forget it's all pretend and fall in love with me." She laughed, a low, husky laugh that sounded like it was meant to seduce. It told Amber that the woman meant every word.

Out of the applicant's sight, she scratched a tiny X on the woman's resume. "Thank you for coming, Miss Tavish. We'll call you if we need you."

"That's it? I thought the interview would have been longer. Don't you have a script you'd like me to read from, so I can demonstrate my acting skills?"

"No, no. That's not necessary." Amber was rising as she spoke, she was that eager to get rid of the woman.

It was a reluctant Tanya Tavish who went through the door. She probably realized that she wasn't exactly a favorite and definitely not a shoe-in. Without realizing it, she'd hammered the first nail into her own coffin when she'd revealed her intentions, daring to mention love as possibly being part of the scenario. As far as Amber was concerned, that was not going to happen. Ever.

Candidate three was perfect. Too perfect. A blonde wearing a demure bob, the way she carried herself and the way she spoke told Amber she was a good fit for Jordan. Quiet, reserved and well-spoken, she looked like the kind of woman who would represent her man well, but would blend into the background when not needed. More than that, she seemed the submissive type, just the sort he'd asked her to find. This was not a woman who would step out of line.

Under normal circumstances Amber's job would be over, but these were not normal circumstances. How would she sleep for the week Jordan would be away, knowing that he was in the company of Miss Right? And although this woman hadn't mentioned love, there was always that possibility.

She gave Miss Temple a reassuring smile. "Thank you for coming," she told her as she walked her to the door. "We'll be in touch within the next few days."

And that was that.

That evening when Jordan called her into his office for an update, she had no candidate to present. Instead, she had a proposal.

As she sank onto the chair across from his desk, she tightened her lips and looked directly into his eyes. "I'm sorry, Jordan, but I could not find a suitable candidate."

That seemed to surprise him. "How is that possible? You told me you had over a hundred responses to the ad."

"I did, but I had a problem with the quality of the applicants."

He frowned. "Maybe you should have tried an agency."

She shrugged. "Maybe." She drew in a steadying breath and then she plunged right in. "I have another idea. Sheikh Ali doesn't know me. What if I come along and play the part of your wife? I know you better than any actor off the street ever could." She held her breath, waiting for his response. If he laughed in her face, she would just die.

His gaze narrowed. "You? You would do that?"

Oh, Lord. What was he thinking? That she was some sort of nut?

She swallowed, her gaze beginning to falter. "I just think it will be easier for me to pull it off, seeing that I've worked for you for over a year and I know you so well."

The sudden curl of his lips made her bite down on her bottom lip. "You know me so well," he said, repeating her words, his voice suddenly soft and strangely seductive. "That's good to know."

But then, as if that intimate moment had never happened, he straightened in his chair, his demeanor back to being the perfect professional. "Thank you for that suggestion." His voice was clipped and cool. "That's not a bad idea at all. It's believable. If it were to ever get out that you work for me, most people understand that office romances will often lead to marriage. I'm sure we can pull it off."

Amber raised her eyebrows. She dared lift her gaze back to his. That had been easier than she'd expected. She'd thought she would have to sell Jordan on the idea of having her play the part of his wife, but he'd accepted it without question. If she'd known it would've been this easy she wouldn't have bothered with the drama of taking all those applications and doing interviews.

But her hesitation in making the suggestion had also been because she'd been scared, so scared that Jordan would find out how she felt about him. And even though she'd finally braved up to offer herself for his role play she would have to be careful...oh, so careful. If Jordan ever found out what was in her heart it would be over. From what she knew of him, how ruthless he could be, she had no doubt that he would not suffer a sentimental fool lightly.

She was still considering that, when his next words jerked her out of her reverie.

"Considering what I'm going to ask of my pretend wife, I'm glad I'll have a companion as competent as you."

Eyes widening at his words, she could only stare back at him. What on earth did he plan to ask of his pretend wife?

***

After Amber left his office, Jordan sat back in his seat and smiled. Things had worked out a lot better than he'd expected.

When he'd given her that story about needing a pretend wife he'd meant it. Sort of. Yes, he'd told Khalil that he had a wife and yes, he'd told him he would be taking her to Dubai with him. But there were ways of getting around that. He could have told the sheikh that his wife was indisposed. He could have said she was traveling, gone to visit her parents, something of substance that would have seemed important enough for her not to be able to make the trip. He hadn't done that, though. Instead, he'd come up with the idea of taking a pretend wife with him.

And he'd had an ulterior motive.

Even though he'd advised Amber to post an announcement and find him a wife, he'd had no intention of taking any other woman but her. A psychologist he was not, but he'd heard about reverse psychology and decided to try it out on her. He knew he might be wrong but he had the feeling she liked him. There were times when she thought he hadn't noticed but he'd caught her peeping at him out of the corner of her eye. Even so, he'd been nothing but professional with Amber Lee. He would never let it be said that he'd abused his position of power and forced his attentions on an unwilling party.

But he'd been interested. More than interested, if he should admit to himself. He downright desired Amber Lee, so badly that there was many a day when he sat there in his office, picturing her in his bed. The girl was a dangerous dose of distraction, that was for sure.

But she was a desirable delicacy he could not resist. If lady luck was on his side, the week-long trip to Dubai, the time they would spend playing such an intimate role, would be the time when her demure reserve would melt and he would have his chance to show her how he truly felt.

And how had he known she would volunteer for the part? He hadn't. He had a back-up plan. No matter what woman she'd presented to him, he would have rejected her. He would have played cranky customer till she'd have gotten so frustrated she would have seen that no-one would satisfy him. No one except her.

Luckily, it hadn't come to that. Like she'd read his mind, like she'd known what lay in his heart, Amber had taken that step he'd been praying for, all this time. She'd decided to be the one.

But he would have to tread very carefully. The girl was like a skittish colt you had to treat with kid gloves. She looked like she scared easily. One wrong move and it would be all over.

As hard as it would be, he would take it slow. And it would be hard, of that he was certain. How could it not, when he could feel himself grow hard, just thinking about her?

It was hard to resist Amber's beauty. Soft waves of dark-blonde hair framed a heart-shaped face. Her succulent pink lips, sometimes pouting when she was deep in concentration, sometimes softly parted, made him want to kiss her...so badly, it hurt. But it was her eyes, those brooding brown eyes that did him in. It was the look he saw in those eyes that made him want to take her in his arms and show her the depth of his desire.

But it would have to wait. He would do absolutely nothing unless she wanted it.

But he had a plan. And if things worked out according to that plan, if he'd read her right and she was truly attracted to him, she would want it. She would want it bad.

# CHAPTER TWO

Dubai was everything Amber thought it would be, and more. Even though it was almost eleven o'clock at night, the city was a beauty to behold. The skyline was breathtaking, and when they entered the city it was equally as impressive. Majestic buildings reached up to the sky, the innovative architecture making her stare, the lights rivaling the beauty of a star-lit sky.

She was entranced. She'd heard about the beauty of this Middle Eastern city but never in her wildest dreams had she imagined that it would be so beautiful. As the limousine took her from the airport to their hotel, she hardly spoke. She was too busy staring out the window at the scenes flitting by. It was all so different, almost surreal, but at the same time, so right.

It wasn't until they were checking in that Amber realized how tired she was. At the reception desk she was standing behind Jordan, stifling a yawn, when she heard something that made her jerk wide awake. "Your ultra suite has a heart-shaped king-sized bed," the desk clerk was saying, "and, of course, the en suite is spacious, with shower stall, tub and Jacuzzi, perfect for a newly married couple."

King-sized bed? Jacuzzi for a newly married couple? What happened to the separate bedrooms she'd booked? Amber reached out to tap Jordan's shoulder. "Uhm, excuse me, but I think there's been a mistake."

To her surprise, he shrugged her off. "We'll talk when we get upstairs," he said, then turned back to the uniformed woman who was smiling at him.

Peeved at the slight, Amber stepped away and even when Jordan beckoned to her to follow him toward the elevator she did not speak to him. The journey to the twenty-fourth floor took longer than she wanted. The whole time she was in the elevator, she was seething. How dare Jordan make changes to the reservation without consulting her?

It wasn't until they walked into the bedroom suite that Amber said a word. She cleared her throat and turned to face her boss. "Jordan," she said, her voice tight, "I didn't know that you'd changed the hotel reservation. Why would you do that?"

He didn't answer until he'd closed the door behind them then dropped his briefcase onto the sofa. "When I realized what you'd done, I made the change. At the last minute," he said as he reached a hand up to loosen his tie. "You'd already left the office so I handled it myself."

Still confused, she pressed him further. "But why did you think the change was necessary?"

He smiled. "Now how would it look if Am Khalil found out we were staying in separate suites? That wouldn't be very convincing, would it?

"But he wouldn't find out-"

Jordan smiled. "You don't know Khalil. He makes it his business to know everybody else's business. And now that I'm here in Dubai, especially mine." Then he laughed and headed toward the kitchenette.

"Don't worry about it," he told Amber as he walked away. "This may be the bridal suite but you're one hundred percent safe with me. There's nothing that's going to happen here...unless you want it to."

The pause in his softly spoken statement was not lost on Amber. Unless she wanted it to? Had he somehow figured out how she felt?

She didn't get a chance to dwell on that, though. He'd come to a halt at the entrance to the kitchenette, turned and was gazing back at her. "Wine?"

She blinked, still tormented by her troubling thoughts. "Y...yes. Thank you."

She could do with some fortification. Maybe wine would do the trick.

But it wasn't long before Amber realized that wine was the last thing she needed just then. When Jordan had brought the wine she'd taken it gratefully, gulping it down so fast she almost choked. Seeing her with an empty glass, he'd refilled it. Desperate for this crutch that could help her collect her wits, she'd quickly consumed the second glass as well. She'd started on her third when she realized the folly of her actions. She'd been a teetotaler all her life. She wasn't used to this sudden intake of alcohol. That, combined with the fact that she was imbibing on an empty stomach, was a real recipe for disaster.

It wasn't long before she realized her mistake. Ready to retire…it was almost midnight, after all…she got up from the sofa, only to find the room spinning around her.

Dazed, she put out a hand to steady herself, a soft moan escaping her lips.

She would have toppled over for sure but, quick as a flash, Jordan was by her side.

"Are you okay?" He put his arms around her as she swayed, steadying her against him. "You only had a couple of glasses. Was that enough to do you in?"

It felt so good, standing there with Jordan's arms wrapped around her, her yielding body pressed against his solid one, that Amber sagged against him and sighed. She began to speak, wanting to tell him how good he felt. At least, she tried. She opened her mouth. "You…you." A hiccup brought an abrupt end to that utterance.

"Hush." Jordan squeezed her even closer, making her melt again the warmth of him. "Time to get you to bed."

"Bed," she whispered, as she melted some more. That sounded so good. She was going to bed, and with Jordan Masters, the man who made her tingle each time he glanced her way. A soft smile slipped onto her lips. It was going to be a glorious night. She had no doubt about that.

Unsteady as she was on her feet, Amber was grateful when her solid source of support bent down and lifted her off her feet and into his arms. "Jordan," she gasped and clung to his sturdy shoulders. "What are you doing?" She'd asked the question in a breathless whisper but she was no fool. She knew exactly what he was doing. He was whisking her off to the suite's bedroom to make mad love to her. The thought made her toes curl in anticipation.

As Jordan crossed the massive bedroom with her in his arms, Amber laid her cheek against his chest and drew in a deep breath, the sensual scent of his cologne making her moan.

His arms tightened around her. "Are you all right?"

Her answer was a soft sigh of satisfaction. They weren't even in bed yet, but Jordan's nearness was making her tremble all over.

As he stepped over to the king-sized bed and gently laid her down, she closed her eyes. With a soft sigh, she let her arms slide away from his shoulders. As she sank against the pillows she drew in a soft breath, her face tilting up, lips parting softly as she awaited his kiss.

And waited.

Seconds passed. Nothing. A fleeting frown settling on her forehead, Amber let her eyelids flutter open to find Jordan standing by the bed, frowning down at her.

She gazed back at him, confused. "Aren't you coming to bed?" she asked, her words a hesitant whisper.

Instead of the smile she was expecting, or even a lifting of the frown on his face, the wrinkle on Jordan's forehead only deepened.

"This is my fault," he said, his voice tight. "I should have guessed you're not used to this."

Then, his face still half hidden in the shadows, he reached out to place a gentle hand on her shoulder. "My apologies, Amber. Get some sleep. You'll be back to your old self by morning."

And with that, he stepped away and walked out of the bedroom, leaving her lying in the shadows. Alone.

Still floating in her wine-induced fog, Amber's mixed-up mind made her spirit sink. What had just happened? She'd waited so long, wanting so badly for Jordan Masters to notice her, to take her in his arms, and she'd finally found the courage to lay her secret bare before him - she wanted him, plain and simple - and he'd rejected her. He'd turned around and walked away.

After that, no matter that Jordan had instructed her to go to sleep, with all that was weighing on her mind she knew she would not have that pleasure, not for a long, long time.

***

Jordan gritted his teeth, feeling guilty as sin.

The minute Amber had agreed to be his pretend wife, his mind had started ticking. She'd given him the chance of a lifetime, one he'd been waiting for all this time, and he'd gone and messed it up.

Although it hadn't been his intention, he'd gotten the girl drunk. And, to his astonishment, she'd offered herself to him.

It had been tempting to take her up on her offer, he wouldn't deny that, but he couldn't. There was no way he would have been able to live with himself if he'd taken advantage of her moment of weakness.

And so, as disappointing as it had been, he'd walked away, kicking himself with every step he took.

In the end, though, as he lay on the sofa, he knew he'd made the right move. When he finally got Amber Lee in his bed...and it would happen, he had no doubt about that...it would be at the perfect moment, when she was totally aware of exactly what was happening. When she came to him she would be willing and, even more important, she would be wanting him in both body and mind.

The thought made him groan. That moment had better be soon. It was going to be torture, lying in the same bedroom suite as Amber, so close but yet so far.

Another soft groan escaping his lips, Jordan closed his eyes then laid a hand on top of the burgeoning bulge in the front of his pants. As rock solid as it was, he was going to have a hard time getting to sleep tonight.

Thinking of Amber lying alone in that big bed? Torture.

# CHAPTER THREE

It was a subdued and silent Amber who traveled in the limo with Jordan Masters that morning.

She was having a hard time finding the courage to meet his gaze. What had she been thinking, throwing herself at him like that? What must he think of her now? Even worse, why hadn't he responded to her unspoken plea? Wasn't he attracted to her, even a little bit? The thought that he had no feelings for her, that he saw her simply as a worker and not as a woman, was the most devastating of all.

The thought making her mood morose, Amber gazed out the window as they were whisked through the streets of Dubai. She did not glance Jordan's way until they arrived at Allied Airlines, the office of his uncle, Sheikh Ali.

When he made as if to help her out of the car, Amber demurred. Jordan could be detached and professional on this business trip? Well, she could be just as cool.

Minutes later, her calm demeanor was put to the test when Jordan laid a gentle hand on her back and urged her toward a tall and stately man wearing a stark white tunic and turban.

"Am Khalil," Jordan said, "I'm happy to present my wife."

At the sound of the words that left Jordan's lips, Amber's heart skipped a beat. His wife. That would be a dream come true. If only it were real.

Quickly, she gathered her thoughts and tilted her head in a polite bow to the smiling man. "I'm pleased to meet you, sir." Not knowing what was expected of her, her voice was soft as she dropped her gaze.

She was shocked when she heard his warm chuckle. "There is no need to be shy, my dear. You are family." His smile widened. "Welcome to Dubai."

She glanced up at him. "Thank you." It was the cordial light in his eyes that put her at ease, making her smile back. "I'm happy to be here."

Later that morning, as the men prepared to talk business, she got more good news. While Jordan was in his meeting, she would be entertained by Riyanne, the sheikh's daughter. This cousin of Jordan was one of the most beautiful women Amber had ever seen, with a heart-shaped face, high cheekbones and full, pouty lips that would put Angelina Jolie to shame. But it was her eyes, shockingly hazel with flecks of gold, that made Amber blink and look twice.

She was almost caught staring but then the girl broke the spell with a warm smile and a nod of her head. "Welcome to Dubai," she said, repeating the words that her uncle had uttered just minutes before. "I will take good care of you today. Would you like something to drink? Some tea, maybe?" As she spoke she was ushering Amber down the hallway and toward the elevator. "I shall take you up to the private lounge," Riyanne said. "There, you can relax and we can talk. I will tell you all about the U. A. E."

"United Arab Emirates," Amber said as she walked with her.

"That is correct. I will tell you all about my country. You are part of the family. You are one of us now. You have a lot to learn." The cheeky smile that slipped onto her lips was so unexpected that Amber raised her eyebrows. It was like Riyanne had something up her sleeve, she knew not what. But in the very little time that she'd known this girl, there was only one adjective that sprang to mind. Naughty. Why that word should come to her, she had no clue.

What she found out, though, and soon enough, was that Riyanne was a whole lot more fun than she would ever have imagined. Up in the luxurious private suite of Allied Airlines, the girl let her hair down, both literally and figuratively.

Throwing off her headscarf, she let her long black hair tumble down her back. Then she walked over to the curved plush sofa and plopped down on top. "Come sit by me," she said. "This is your home, too. Make yourself comfortable."

The girl was so welcoming that Amber was quick to take her up on her offer. She was glad for the opportunity to relax, and especially with someone who was so open and friendly, so willing to accept a virtual stranger into her private space.

When she settled down, Riyanne gave her a pat on the arm. "I will be right back," she said. "I will get you a cup of chamomile tea." She raised her eyebrows at Amber. "Yes? That is good for you?"

Amber gave her a grateful nod. "Very good," she said, smiling as her hostess hopped up and headed for another room in the suite. She guessed she was going to the kitchen.

Within minutes Riyanne was back, bearing a tray with cups and tiny plates on which sat slices of pastry. She laid the tray on top of the coffee table then turned to Amber. "I will tell you about my country," she said, repeating what she'd said earlier, "and then there is something I want to show you." The naughty gleam was back in her eyes. "You are a married woman now, my cousin's wife. There are things you must know." Slowly, she shook her head. "You are his wife but you are a foreigner. I do not think you have yet been schooled. There are things you must know, to please your man." She clasped her hands together, the cheeky smile back on her lips. "Do not worry. I will teach you what you will need to know."

That made Amber blink. "Teach me what I need to know?" What had she walked into? A harem school of sorts? Here she was, thinking that she'd come to this office to meet only a stern and staid man and instead she'd been placed in the hands of a young woman who was obviously anxious to teach her how to take her 'marriage' to a whole new level.

Shocked at the turn of events, that the sheikh's niece was not the demure and meek maiden she had expected, Amber shifted on the sofa as Riyanne took a seat beside her.

"Let us have some tea," the girl said. "There is much I have to tell you."

She was actually relieved when Riyanne's conversation centered around the people, the country and the culture. That, she could handle. She soon relaxed in Riyanne's presence, grateful for all she was learning. She'd had no clue that Dubai was the only place in the world with a seven star hotel, and that more than eighty percent of its population were immigrants. Even more interesting was the fact that earnings were tax free. In the end, Amber was glad that Riyanne had stolen her away from the men. She'd learned so much from this bubbly young woman, things the men probably would not have shared with her.

But there was more...

As soon as they'd finished eating, the girl hopped up again. "I will be right back," she said. "There is something I must show you." With that, she turned and hurried out of the room.

Curiosity making her bite her lip, Amber clasped her hands in her lap and sat back in the sofa to wait. She did not have to wait long. What she saw made her gasp.

Riyanne was walking toward her and what she was wearing would make any man salivate. Dressed in a diaphanous garment that revealed the length of her legs and the curve of her breasts, Riyanne was a strikingly seductive sight that had Amber's jaw dropping.

"Wow." The weak whisper was as much as she could muster. She could hardly believe this was the same woman who had left the room. Gone was the modest maiden. In her place was a tantalizing temptress who turned kohl-lined eyes toward her.

A sly smile slipped onto Riyanne's lips. "Ready for your lecture in Arabian ardor?"

Amber swallowed. The girl was serious. Slowly, she nodded and then, her throat tight, she croaked out her answer.

"Ready when you are."

***

Amber could not believe she was in Dubai, sitting on a sofa, eagerly awaiting a lesson on playing the part of the perfect wife. And from a fresh-face girl, at that. At her ripe age of twenty-six, Amber felt like a matron around Riyanne. The girl could not have been older than nineteen or twenty, yet she was offering to train her in matrimony. Didn't that beat all.

Riyanne gave her an encouraging smile. "I know this must seem strange, for me to be offering you lessons, but I must be honest with you." She cleared her throat. "Please do not think me forward, but the moment I met you I knew we were sisters." A slight frown wrinkled her forehead. "What do you call it? Soulmates?"

That made Amber tilt her head. "Thank you, but...why?"

Riyanne lifted her shoulders in a shrug. "I do not know. Maybe it is because you seemed so lost, standing there by the side of your husband. Maybe even a little sad. I felt...forgive me...sorry for you."

"Oh." Amber didn't know how to respond to that. But the girl was perceptive, that she could see. Riyanne had read her very quickly, even going so far as to sense her slight sadness. She was impressed. This river ran deeper than she would have expected.

Her newfound friend - or, as Riyanne had put it, her sister - surprised her yet again when she walked over to the sofa, sat down beside her, and took her hand. "You seem so afraid," she said gently. "Please do not be. I know it must be difficult to adjust to married life but it can be wonderful. Just follow my advice and you will be fine."

"Your advice?"

"Yes. I know all about it."

This time Amber could not hold back the chuckle. "You know all about it? You've done this before?"

Riyanne gave her a rueful grin. "I wish that were so. No, better than that, I was schooled by a wise woman from my home in the country. There, in the villages, they spend the time to prepare you. It is not like here." Her lips twisted in a show of disdain. "In the big city no-one has the time to talk with a woman before her wedding, and school her in the ways of women."

Again, curiosity got the better of Amber. "So you were trained in this? Why? Were you preparing for marriage?"

Riyanne nodded. "When I was eighteen I was betrothed to a man my father had chosen for me. In the end, the marriage did not materialize."

Her heart aching in sympathy, Amber squeezed her hand. "I'm so sorry."

Riyanne surprised her with a laugh. "Please do not be. I did not love him and besides, his children are all older than I am. They would have probably been happy to bully me once I moved into their home."

"Oh." It was the second time within the hour that Amber found herself without words.

"Now let us get started." Riyanne released her hand, settled back in the seat and, like she meant business, she folded her arms across her chest.

By the time the girl was done her spiel, Amber knew exactly what it would take to be the perfect wife ...by Riyanne's standards, anyway. Apparently, as a dutiful wife it was essential that you be a good cook, a bearer of bouncing babies, and a source of support when your man was down in the dumps. More than that, it was critical that you played the part of a perfect partner in bed. That was when the lesson got really interesting.

"Do you see what I am wearing?" Riyanne asked. "Do you see how it frames my figure, highlighting my feminine form?"

Amber had to agree that the outfit did that very well.

"This is how you must dress for your man. Such fashions and robes are reserved for the bedroom. This is where it is your duty to tempt him and please him." Then she went into a vivid account of how to achieve just that, a level of detail which was enough to make Amber blush. By the time the girl was done, she was feeling hot under the collar. Goodness.

"You do not wish your husband to take a second wife, do you?" Riyanne was practically glaring at her.

"Uh, no. I guess not."

"You guess not? Your answer should be, absolutely not. I know you American wives feel that you do not have to worry about these things, but what if your husband decides to move here? Then it would be perfectly legal. You must do whatever you can to satisfy him one hundred percent, in the home but especially in bed. That way he will not be tempted to look at anyone else."

"I...see." Amber didn't know what else to say. This was the strangest conversation she'd ever had.

"I have something for you." Riyanne patted her on the knee then she got up. "What I will give you will have him wanting you so much he will not be able to keep his hands off you."

Amber swallowed but she said not a word. It sounded good, having Jordan wanting her that much, but this was also getting a bit scary. What if she tried Riyanne's tricks and he turned around and rejected her?

She was not too surprised when her hostess brought out another of those outfits, what she was now coming to think of as 'harem suits'.

"Luckily, you and I are about the same size." The girl made her stand so she could hold the robe against her body. "Perfect. This one is brand new. Now it is yours."

"No, please. I can't just take your things-"

Riyanne cut her off. "It is yours. If you do not take it, I will be very offended."

Giving in to the pressure, Amber thanked her with a smile and a quick hug. "You are so kind," she murmured. She was beginning to feel overwhelmed by Riyanne's kindness. Uncertain though she was about executing the girl's well-laid plan, she was wiling to try it out.

What did she have to lose...except her dignity?

# CHAPTER FOUR

That evening, Amber couldn't get back to the hotel fast enough. Now that Riyanne had stoked the fire of her desire, she was anxious to make her move on the man who made her melt at the thought of them sharing the bridal bed.

But there was one thing she needed to do before anything else. It was the only way she would be able to find the courage to follow through on her plan. She had to call her best friend back home. Sasha was a newly married woman and her past partner-in-crime. Sasha, crazy girl that she was, would know exactly how to handle the situation.

As soon as she and Jordan got in from dinner at Al Mahara, one of the top restaurants in Dubai, she escaped into the bedroom while he sat in the living room, sipping a glass of wine as he watched the evening news. She'd hardly closed the door behind her before she began dialing the number on her cell phone.

As soon as her friend picked up, she began to speak in an urgent whisper. "Sasha, I need your help. You're going to think I'm so crazy but I've come up with a plan to seduce a man."

She heard Sasha's sharp intake of breath. "What the heck? Seduce a man? What man?"

Amber chuckled softly. "Remember the one man I talk about? The one I told you is always so aloof?"

"What? Your boss?"

"The same. I'm all the way in Dubai. With him."

"You're kidding me." The words came out in an incredulous gasp. "You'd better be. How could you be all the way in Dubai and I don't know about it?"

Amber chuckled again. "That's because I didn't want to tell you the reason I was going. I didn't want to lie to you but I didn't want to tell you the truth, either. If I'd told you where I was going and why, you would have tried to convince me to scrap the whole idea."

"I want to wring your neck, that's what I want to do."

"Okay, okay, but before you do, there's something I need to tell you."

"Did you sleep with him?"

The quick question was such a shock that it left Amber speechless. When she finally answered, it was with a stutter. "N...no, of course not."

"Mmhmm." The skeptical sound told Amber that Sasha did not believe a word of what she was saying.

"I'm serious," she said, trying to make her friend understand. "I've just been schooled in the art of seduction."

"What are you talking about?"

Now that she had Sasha's attention, Amber decided to fill her in. "I'm here in Dubai for one reason," she said. "I'm here as Jordan Masters' pretend wife."

"What the heck?" It was Sasha's favorite phrase. Amber was not surprised that she'd already used it twice in their conversation. The situation certainly called for it.

She sighed. "I know it sounds weird but when I explain you'll see that it makes a lot of sense." She immediately launched into the details and even when she heard Sasha's incredulous gasps and groans, she did not pause until she'd told all. Only then did she pause to pose her question. "Now do you see why I had to do it? I had no choice."

Sasha clicked her tongue, not sounding at all impressed with the story she'd just heard. "You did not have to do that, Amber, and you know it. You and I know that the only reason you grabbed onto this crazy scheme is because you're head over heels in love with that man. Crazy."

Amber sighed. "Crazy or not, I need your help. You're a married woman now. I want you to tell me if my plan would be more of a turn-off than a turn-on." Sasha's silence told her she was all ears. Encouraged by that, she proceeded to share the scheme she and Riyanne had cooked up, what they'd concluded was the perfect plan to get Jordan totally hooked. It was a bit embarrassing, telling Sasha about her seduction scheme, but who else could she confide in? Swallowing her embarrassment, she kept on talking, not pausing until she'd told all.

"So what do you think?" The question came out as a tentative whisper.

Still silence. Finally, Sasha let out a soft groan. "It's a crazy plan," she said. "So crazy it just might work." Then she chuckled. "When you're done with him he'll probably be groveling at your feet. With a plan like that, by the time you get back to California your position as pretend wife will be part of the past. He'll ask you to marry him, for sure.

Her throat tight, Amber could not respond. It was exactly what she was hoping but she knew the chances were super slim. How do you get a man from hardly noticing you, to falling in love and asking you to marry him, all within the space of a week-long business trip?

Sasha began speaking again, cutting into her thoughts. "You've got a plan, girl," she said. "Now go work it."

"All right, I will."

Even after she'd hung up the phone, Sasha's words of encouragement still rang in her ears, buoying her spirits as she pulled out the sexy outfit. Determined to carry out her scheme, she did not linger. Minutes later she was sliding her palms over her breasts as she bathed her body in the scented oils Riyanne had given her.

Satisfied with the seductive power of the sweet scent, Amber slipped into the super sensual suit her newfound friend had given her. Immediately, she was transformed. Dressed in the semi-transparent, form-fitting suit, there was no sign of the demure woman who had visited the offices of Allied Airlines that day. In her place was a timid-looking temptress. She frowned at herself in the mirror. Timid? She would fix that soon enough.

Armed with her cosmetics bag, Amber got down to business. Within minutes she was a new woman, one she herself hardly recognized. Kohl-lined eyes staring back at her, she lifted the liner to her lips then painted the softness in ruby-red, a striking contrast to the paleness of her skin. The color, so bold, was the perfect match for the ruby sash that cinched her waist.

She slipped her feet into the soft satin slippers that Riyanne had given her then, last of all, she lifted the sheer swathe of soft Japanese silk, letting it float down to fall on top of her head, to cover the dark blonde waves of her hair. As the feather-light fabric floated around her shoulders she drew one end of the veil across the lower half of her face, obscuring the freshly painted lips, exposing the mascara-heavy, carefully contoured eyes. It was such a seductive sight, the lips hidden, only the curve of her cheekbones and the bold eyes bare to the gaze. How could Jordan resist?

Satisfied with her handiwork, she drew in a shaky breath then let it out on a sigh. "Well, here goes," she whispered, then turned toward the door.

***

"Come on, come on."

Jordan was sitting on the sofa, so caught up in the basketball game that he almost did not respond when he glimpsed the slight movement from the corner of his eye. "Yes!" He was practically hopping up off the sofa. It was the three-pointer that clinched the game, and not a second too soon. And, after rooting for the Lakers for almost two hours, he could finally relax into the warm glow of victory.

His lips still parted in a grin, he shifted his gaze to the figure standing in the doorway.

What he saw made his jaw drop.

Was that Amber? The woman standing there in the doorway, hand on hip in the most seductive pose, was one of the most beautiful sights he'd ever seen. "Oh, wow." The soft gasp of astonishment escaped his lips as he stared at the siren standing there, smiling at him. "What happened to you?" His words weak with wonder, he tilted his head as he gazed at the vision of loveliness leaning against the door jamb.

Her response was to walk toward him, her hips swaying in a rhythm so sensual he could not tear his eyes away from her. Not that he wanted to.

Clothed in her suit of fabric so light it was almost transparent, Amber came to stand before him, the curve of her hips and her breasts visible to his gaze.

It was enough to make his member rigid as a rod.

Not sure where she was going with this, he waited for Amber to make the next move.

And move, she did. Like she was hearing the sultry sounds of music, she began to sway, her hips rocking then rotating in a rhythm that had his gaze glued to her. She was moving like she was a natural. He could not believe this was the reserved woman he knew.

As he gazed up at her Amber leaned forward, filling his nostrils with a most seductive fragrance. He had to bite back a groan.

As he closed his eyes, all the better to revel in her nearness, Amber whispered in his ear. "We have the perfect arrangement," she said, her voice suggestive in its sultriness, "for me to give you the perfect pleasure. You are my husband, are you not?"

All he could do was nod. Right at that moment it did not matter that their marriage was no more than a sham. All he could think about was the pleasure he'd been promised. His mouth dry, he licked his lips in anticipation.

And speaking of licking, it was like he'd transmitted his lecherous thoughts to the lady leaning over him. She tilted her head toward him then, her lips sliding along the length of his neck, she began to lick at the surface of skin just below his ear, sending shivers shimmering up his spine.

"Oh, jeez."

His soft sigh seemed to spur her on. Pressing her palms to his shoulders she gave him a gentle shove, making him fall back against the back of the sofa. Before he could react she was climbing on top of him, straddling his lap, making him moan when the softness of her derrière connected with the hardness of his groin.

"Oh, God." As the guttural groan left his lips he reached up to clasp the tiny waist and pull her closer. It was almost too much, the tempting and teasing of that impromptu massage brought on by her movement as she shifted on his lap.

He was sucking in a shaky breath when, her warm breath tickling his ear, she whispered again. "Are you ready," she whispered, "to help me fulfill my fantasy?"

"What fantasy?" Whatever it was, right then fulfilling a fantasy sounded like a damn good idea.

Now she was feathering soft kisses along the side of his face, distracting him so he could hardly speak.

"That fantasy that all men have," she said. "You want me as your love slave, don't you? You want to tie me up and ravish me."

Jordan could not believe what he was hearing. It sounded good, but where had this tigress come from? Horny though he was, even with those wicked words still ringing in his ears, he decided to play it safe.

Instead of picking up his petite temptress and taking her back to the bedroom, he reached his hands up to cup her cheeks.

"Is this what you want?" he asked. "For me to take you to bed and ravish you?" *Say, yes. Please, say yes.*

He was watching her intently, holding her face in his hands, making her unable to turn away. He saw when she swallowed, her tongue darting out to nervously lick her lips. "Y..yes. I want what you want."

He did not release her face. "Don't worry about what I want. The question is, what do you want? Why are you doing this?" He saw her hesitation. "Look at me."

The firm command worked. Her eyelids fluttered then she lifted her gaze to his.

"Why are you doing this?" he asked again.

"Because I want you to l-" She stopped abruptly then bit her lip. "Because this is what all men want. A seductress at your disposal. Right?" Like she wasn't sure, her eyelids fluttered and she dropped her gaze again.

That was when Jordan knew. Amber might be playing the part of temptress and doing a good job of it, too, but she was not ready. Far from it. The uncertainty in her eyes was all he needed to see, to know he had to go slow.

As much as he wanted her - so badly, it hurt - he was not going to go down that road, not until she was one hundred percent ready.

He decided to tell her just that. "You're not ready for this, Amber. Let's just relax and have a quiet evening together, okay?"

It hurt to see her face fall. He would have wanted nothing else but to fulfill the fantasy she'd expressed. But it was not the right time.

As his hands fell away from her face, her prettily painted lips formed into a pout and she slid off his lap, looking like she wanted to get as far away from him as she could.

The frown on her face told of the depth of her disappointment. As she turned away, he heard her soft murmur. "I should never have listened to Riyanne. What does she know about men?"

That got his attention. "Riyanne? What does she have to do with this?"

"Nothing."

Before he could question her further, Amber turned and fled into the bedroom, closing the door behind her, but not before he heard a soft hiccup that sounded suspiciously like a sob.

Jordan folded his arms across his chest as he settled back against the sofa, his mind mulling over Amber's softly spoken words.

Riyanne Ali. He frowned at the thought of his cousin. He should never have agreed for Amber to hang out with her. His cousin had been known to get into all sorts of trouble. When she was little, her naughtiness would often put the boys to shame.

As his frown deepened, he tightened his lips. Tomorrow he would have a talk with his little cousin.

Before that day was over, he would get to the bottom of the dramatic transformation of his pretend bride.

# CHAPTER FIVE

Amber opened her eyes to a stream of golden light breaching the barrier of the damask drapes drawn at the window. Instead of her usual eagerness to get started on a new day, her reaction was a soft groan. The memories rushing back, she turned her face and pressed it into the pillow. Talk about embarrassing. How would she face Jordan after she'd humiliated herself like she had, throwing herself at him, only to be rejected?

It did not bear thinking about.

Humiliated beyond belief, for several minutes she just lay there, wallowing in misery and self-pity. Then, knowing that he would soon be knocking on the bedroom door, she rolled out of bed and headed for the bathroom. She certainly didn't need to add to her embarrassment by giving him an uncensored view of her pillow-wrinkled face and tousled hair.

She was standing in front of the bathroom mirror, toweling her hair, when she heard a knock at the bedroom door. Quickly, she grabbed one of the robes hanging from the hooks on the back of the bathroom door and wrapped it around her. She was tying the sash tightly around her in an almost defensive mode as she headed toward the bedroom door.

As she opened it she dropped her gaze. "Good morning," she mumbled. "It's all yours." She stepped aside to let him in, expecting him to make a beeline for the bathroom.

When he just stood there, she lifted her gaze to find him looking at her, a slight frown on his forehead. "Are you okay?" he asked.

"I'm fine," she snapped. "Why?"

"You look...tired." He glanced over at the bed, probably to check if she'd slept. The pillows were still out of place, the covers thrown back. At the sight of it all, his frown lifted and he stepped into the bedroom. Then, with a nod, he turned and walked toward the bathroom.

Jordan could not get there fast enough, as far as Amber was concerned. As soon as the bathroom door closed behind him she made a dash for the closet, ripped business suit and blouse off the hangers and threw them on top of the bed. She ripped off her robe and within seconds she was wearing underwear and stockings, then she was slipping into pencil-slim skirt and buttoning up her blouse. By the time a slick-haired, robe-wearing Jordan emerged from the steamy bathroom, she was sitting on the side of the freshly made bed, calmly pulling a comb through her curls. Or, at least, pretending to be calm.

The sexy sight of him was almost her undoing. He hadn't tied his robe as tightly as she had, and it had fallen open at the top to reveal a broad chest covered in a light matte of dark, curly hair. His frame, too tall for the robe, had the fabric falling some inches above his knees, to reveal muscled thighs that tapered to strong shins on which shone slick and wet, the same dark curls that covered his chest.

It took a moment for Amber to realize that she was staring. His near nakedness making her pulse pick up pace, she dropped her gaze and turned her face away, but not before she'd glimpsed the smug smile that slipped onto his lips.

He'd caught her staring. He could probably guess the effect his presence was having on her. That was why he was gloating. The beast.

After that, she resolved that there was nothing Jordan could do that would get under her skin. More than that, there was nothing he could do, no matter how he affected her, that would make her offer herself to him and humiliate herself again. Not happening. Not in this lifetime or the next.

Her mind made up, Amber screwed up her courage and faced her foe head on, fixing him with cold stares when he later tried to make conversation, sitting silent as the limousine whisked them through the city, barely acknowledging him as he helped her out of the car. It wasn't until they were standing in front of his uncle that she forced a smile.

Feeling the strain of her self-imposed silence, Amber was more than relieved when Riyanne came to rescue her.

"We will leave the men to their meetings," the girl said. "You and I, we have much to discuss." Amber didn't miss the secret wink the girl gave her.

Minutes later, safe in the private suite of Allied Airlines, Amber let out a long, slow sigh and sank onto the softness of the sofa.

"So how did you fare?" Riyanne didn't beat around the bush. With her quick question she cut to the chase, gazing eagerly at Amber as she sat on the other end of the sofa. "Were you successful in winning him over, making him want you more than anything in the world?"

Amber grimaced. "Not...really."

Riyanne stared back at her, looking perplexed. "What does that mean? The dance, the body oils. My plan of seduction. Did they not work?"

Amber grimaced again. "Not...really."

Now Riyanne looked even more confused. "Please explain."

Totally embarrassed, Amber cleared her throat. Where to begin? It wasn't like Riyanne was some kind of counselor. She was just a girl, trying out seduction techniques she'd learned or heard about. Why should she tell her anything?

But, going against her gut, Amber began to speak. It was like she had to lighten the load that weighed so heavily on her mind. "It didn't work," she admitted, feeling shame sweeping over her. Imagine having to admit her failure to a girl all of six or seven years younger than she was.

Frowning, Riyanne tilted her head. "What happened?"

Amber let out a puff of air. "I wore the costume, like you told me. I even did that special dance you taught me."

"And the body oils?"

Amber nodded. "That, too." Then she shook her head. "Nothing."

Riyanne's frown deepened. "What do you mean, nothing?"

Amber's lips twisted in self-deprecation. "I mean, I did everything right - the dress, the oils, the dance - and he still rejected me. He didn't want me." Her words ended on a bitter note that made her bite her lip.

But Riyanne's next question made her realize she'd made a big mistake. "He rejected you? His wife?"

Oh, Lord. How was she going to explain that? She tossed around in her mind for an answer that would make sense. When she began, her voice was slow, hesitant. "What I meant was, he wasn't as excited as I expected. He acted like it was...normal. I thought he would have been so surprised and happy that he would have...he would have..."

Riyanne gave her a look of understanding. "You don't have to say it. I know what you mean. He is not a man who is easily seduced. He will be, how do you say, a lot of work."

Glad for the explanation Riyanne volunteered, Amber was quick to agree. "Yes, that's exactly it. He is my husband but he is hard to seduce. He is too...straitlaced."

Riyanne seemed to buy that story because she nodded, her look grave. And then her brows fell, her lips tightening in a sign of determination. "We will not give up," she said tersely. "Not that easily. We will try another tactic. By the time we are through with your husband, you will have him on his knees."

Amber had no idea what that meant but she was all ears. "What do you have in mind?" she dared ask.

Riyanne hopped up off the sofa and began to pace the floor, her brow wrinkled in concentration. "You must be more aggressive," she said, her voice firm. "No more Mrs., what do you call it, Mrs. Nice Guy. Some men are not captivated by a woman who is too soft and yielding. Some men want a dominant woman, one who can master them. That's what you must be."

Now it was Amber's turn to frown. "A dominatrix?"

Riyanne stopped her pacing long enough to throw her a smile. "No, not like that." She shook her head. "Nothing like that. Like a lady."

That made Amber lift her eyebrows. "Dominant like a lady, you say. I think you'd better tell me how that works."

Several minutes later, after a lengthy lesson from Riyanne, Amber realized that the dominant lady scheme might work very well. She'd gotten her feet wet with her first attempt at seduction but, compared with what Riyanne was suggesting now, that had been mere kid's play.

"You have to get aggressive," Riyanne was saying. "First, make him jealous, make him angry, get that blood boiling. Then you make your move."

Amber wrinkled her nose. "Sounds kind of dangerous."

Riyanne nodded eagerly. "Now you understand. Danger is a necessary evil. It makes the man take notice. The key is to know how far to go and when to pull back. Now listen to my new plan."

Amber didn't know if she liked the sound of that but curiosity won out. She listened. By the time Riyanne stopped talking she was pumped up and ready to roll.

"I will try that," she said, determination making her feel bold. "For tonight's plan of seduction, aggressive Amber it is.

***

It had been a long day. It wasn't only that he'd been in meetings all morning and then all afternoon. Part of his problem was that Amber had been weighing heavily on his mind.

From the time they'd gotten up that morning and even while they rode to the office she'd been strangely silent, so much so that he'd wondered if he'd done something to offend her. She couldn't be angry because he hadn't taken her up on her offer, could she? She had to understand that it had been for her own good.

At least, he hoped she did. But the way she was acting, it didn't seem that way. Even as they rode in the limo back to the hotel she remained silent, responding to his questions with monosyllabic answers, stealing sly glances his way when she thought he wasn't looking.

Even when they got ready and went out for dinner that evening, she was unusually quiet, nodding and responding pleasantly enough but not making any effort at conversation. And yet, when she thought he wasn't noticing, she would throw quick glances his way, a strangely smug smile stealing onto her lips like she was enjoying a well-kept secret at his expense. Very strange.

Things got even stranger when they got back to the hotel. Rather than seeking out fine dining, at Amber's suggestion they had dinner at one of the restaurants right there at the hotel. As hotel restaurants went, it was elegant enough, not Jordan's first choice but he wasn't picky. Going downstairs to Chic Cuisine was normal enough but it was when they were in the middle of the meal that things got really weird, albeit in a quirky cute way.

It started with a pat on the hand when he dropped his napkin on top of the table, just beside his plate. It was what you could call a 'smart pat'. She'd hit him hard enough that it actually hurt.

"Napkin on your lap," she said, her voice so firm it was kind of funny. She sounded like an old school marm.

"Yes, ma'am." Playing along, he gave her a nod and immediately drew the napkin down to spread it across his lap. He raised an eyebrow at her. "Anything else?"

She cut him a cold glare. "Nothing else. As long as you behave."

Was this some sort of game? Where did Amber get off, looking like she wanted to boss him around? She was beginning to make him feel like a disobedient schoolboy, the way she was acting. Still, he let it slide. It was clear that she had something up her sleeve. He would just play along and make her feel good for the moment. It was a small price to pay to get her in a good mood.

The rest of the meal went fairly smoothly, with Amber playing nice and actually cracking a smile when the server came to refill their glasses with wine. The smile wasn't the problem. It was the look she gave the guy that had Jordan's lips tightening, as he looked from one to the other. The look she was giving the man was pure flirtation. It could be mistaken for nothing else. Without saying a word, she was actually toying with the guy, making a blush creep up his neck, making him stammer his words.

Jordan couldn't believe it. Amber was flirting? Here in Dubai? Right in front of his face? Had did the girl gone mad?

Before she could make any further blunders, he wrapped up the meal real fast, not bothering with dessert, declining the wine the young man was offering him.

He beat a hasty exit, Amber by his side, looking haughty and bold and not at all ashamed of her wayward behavior.

It pissed him off. Big time.

The minute they walked into the suite, the moment the door closed behind them, Jordan confronted Amber. "What the hell was that all about?" His voice was not loud. It didn't have to be. His tone was cold enough for her to get the message. He was mad as hell.

Looking like she couldn't care less, she turned to face him, her demeanor calm and unperturbed. "That," she said coolly, "was your first lesson in obedience."

Jordan blinked, he was so surprised. For a second he was speechless. When he finally spoke, his tone was tight. "What did you say?"

Amber tossed her head, a disdainful move if there ever was one, and folded her arms across her chest. The look she gave him was haughty as hell. Head thrown back, she was practically glaring down her nose at him. "In case you didn't get that, I said that was your first lesson in obedience. You need to learn to listen to your mistress." Back straight, standing as tall as her petite frame would allow, her glare was uncompromising and unapologetic.

What the hell?

Jordan saw red. It was time to teach this little temptress turned tigress a lesson she would not soon forget.

Anger making his breath tight in his throat, Jordan's hands shot out to clasp Amber by the shoulders and haul her close. Even when she gasped, her eyes widening in surprise, he did not let her go. "Lesson in obedience?" he growled. "You're the one learning that lesson tonight."

Before he could give things a second thought, before he could change his mind, adrenaline pumping in his veins, Jordan hauled his captive even closer, his hands reaching out to cup her chin so he could tilt her face up to his. Before she could recover, he lowered his lips to capture hers in a kiss so fierce that soon he had no need to hold her close. She was the one clinging to him.

His anger feeding his passion, Jordan plundered Amber's lips, making her yield to his every demand. So she wanted to show she was boss? By the time he was done with her, she would know soon enough who was really in charge.

Cupping the back of her head in the palm of his hand, Jordan tilted her head, all the better to have access to the sweetness of her lips. He was in control of that kiss, making her moan, letting her learn the lesson she should have been taught a long time ago - what it meant to be a woman, what it meant to yield to the masterful command of a man.

He was reveling in his dominance when it happened. A sharp slap to the side of his face had him jerking back in shock.

His jaw slack, he just had time to jerk his face away before another slap was sent his way. It just missed him. Immediately, he let go of her shoulders and stepped back, out of the line of fire. "What the hell is wrong with you? Have you gone crazy?"

Instead of wilting at his heated words, Amber planted her palms on his chest and shoved, forcing him even farther away from her.

"You've clearly not learned your lesson." Eyes flashing fire, her words were spoken through gritted teeth. "How dare you kiss me without permission? Get over to that sofa. Now."

What the-

He didn't have time to react to her order. Before he could respond, she'd grabbed his arm, her grip stronger than he would have imagined, and was dragging him over to that spot to which she'd ordered him. Far too surprised to resist, he let her drag him there, even letting her shove him in the chest so he tumbled back onto the seat.

Quickly, before he'd recovered, she slipped off her shoes and climbed onto his lap. A growl escaping her lips, she dug her fingers into his hair and yanked his head back, forcing him to gaze up into her frowning face.

That was when he realized what was going on. For some strange reason Amber had gotten it into her head to play the role of dominatrix. It was a one hundred and eighty degree turn from the submissive seductress she'd played the night before. What in blue blazes was going on with his travel companion? It was like some sort of fever had taken over since she'd landed in Dubai.

"Pay attention." A light slap to his cheek cut his musing short. He blinked, his eyes focusing on the face frowning down at him.

As he stared up at her, she hopped off his lap and reached out to grab the collar of his shirt. "Up." She issued the order with a tug at the shirt. "It's off to the shower for you. For what I want to do tonight, I want you washed and squeaky clean."

Bemused, Jordan did not resist. Like the lady ordered, he got up and made a meek exit, crossing the bedroom with Amber in tow. Apparently, his lady was planning on joining him in his ablutions.

Surreptitiously, he licked his lips. It looked like it was going to be an eventful evening.

He was looking forward to it.

# CHAPTER SIX

A pounding heart and sweaty palms were not going to deter Amber. Not tonight. She'd pondered on her plan all day, how to seduce her pseudo-spouse. Her submissive act had not worked. Well, now she was switching things up, taking a totally different tack. The element of surprise would be on her side, a strategy that was sure to yield success. It had better. This time it was do or die. If, after all this, Jordan still decided to reject her, she would never recover. She would never be able to look him in the face again.

In the en suite they came to a halt, Jordan turning to give her a quizzical look.

"Do I undress," he asked, his lips curling in a smirk, "or do I wait for you to do it?" He paused, his smile widening. "Boss?"

Amber's brows fell. She didn't like that. Jordan was enjoying this way too much. Doing her best to look intimidating, she folded her arms across her chest. "Get out of those clothes," she ordered. "Now."

Fortunate for her, he was quick to obey. Maybe a bit too quick, if truth be told. In just a few swift moves, shirt was gone and so were trousers. Before she could avert her gaze he'd hooked his thumbs into the waist of his boxer briefs and was pushing the garment off his hips.

Immediately, that most private part of him sprang into view, leaving her standing there staring, as the color flew up to stain her cheeks. She gulped.

Jordan Masters was a sight to behold. Obviously aroused in his state of undress, his manhood stood firm and strong, jutting away from the bed of soft black hair that curled at his groin. Amber blinked. Then she licked her lips.

*Come on, girl. Don't wimp out now.*

It was a well-needed pep talk. After playing tough all evening and trying to boss Jordan around, there was no way she could afford to show her nervousness. She'd promised Riyanne she would be Aggressive Amber tonight and that was exactly who she intended to be.

Before she chickened out, she turned her back to the beautifully sculpted body that had just graced her view, lifting shaking fingers to the buttons of her blouse. "Get yourself in the shower," she ordered through gritted teeth. "Make sure that water is nice and warm before I get there."

"Yes, ma'am."

Amber was not looking at Jordan but she could just imagine the grin on his face. The tickled tone of his words were testament to his amusement.

It annoyed the heck out of her. She wanted him thrown off balance, not happy as hell. Wanting to regain control, or at least looking like it, Amber let her clothes fall to the floor then drew in a fortifying breath and turned, head high, her gaze bold and unwavering.

It did the trick. Jordan had been watching her and when she stepped into the warm stream of water, her eyes locked on his, her gaze unwavering, his smile faltered. A look of confusion clouded his gaze. She could guess that he'd expected her to be hesitant. Her boldness and calm control were clearly the cause of his confusion.

She grabbed the washcloth from the bar and shoved it under his nose. "Wash me," she ordered.

He obeyed. His glittering gaze never leaving her, he took the cloth from her hand then squeezed the fragrant bath gel onto it. Her heart pounding at the intimacy of his touch, she let him circle her breasts with the foamy fabric then slide it across her shoulders and down her arms. As she closed her eyes, all the better to savor the sensation, he slid the cloth across her chest, down between her breasts then over the soft skin of her torso.

Her breath tight in her throat, Amber clenched her eyes shut, too tense to relax, too taut to steal a glance Jordan's way. All she could do was hold her breath, knowing exactly where he was headed, wanting it, anticipating it, yet fearing it just the same.

Like he knew his purpose and like he intended to fulfill it whatever the cost, Jordan kept going, down, down, until Amber's gasp gave him pause. It was the surest sign that he'd reached his goal.

Tease that he was, Jordan slipped the cloth lower still, sliding it between her legs, sending sweet thrills rippling up her body.

"Ooh." She couldn't help the soft sigh that slipped from her lips. The sensations were sending her senses swirling, making her eyes flutter open as she reached down to grip his wrist. "Please," she whispered. "Wait."

That wasn't exactly what she'd intended to do. She'd meant to be firm. She'd meant to issue a command. But it was so hard to be strong when his intimate caress was making her so weak.

Gathering her strength around her, she tightened her grip around his wrist and forced it away from her. "I will do it," she said, her voice abnormally loud as she struggled to regain her composure. "Turn around."

When he didn't move fast enough she pressed her palm to his shoulder and pushed, making him turn away from her. Then, temporarily shielded from the intensity of his gaze, she proceeded to slide the cloth across his shoulders then down his back. That was bad enough, stroking the strength of his back, following the cloth as it slid over the hard muscles and smooth skin

But it soon got worse for Amber. A whole lot worse. How was a girl to keep her wits about her when, right in front of her, was the most delectable derrière she'd ever seen?

Jordan Masters had the most beautiful butt Amber had ever seen on a man. Not that she'd seen many, but you didn't have to see a lot to know that this was one of the best - toned, firm yet smooth to the touch. His was a man butt that would make any woman tempted to touch.

And touch she did...hesitantly at first, sliding the soapsuds over his skin, then more boldly, massaging his muscles as she stroked.

His involuntary moan making her bold, Amber reached out to grip the firmness of his hip, urging him till he'd turned to face her again, giving her a full frontal view of his figure. And what a view it was.

For a swift second Amber closed her eyes tight, overwhelmed by his nearness, the sight of him, the manly scent of him. But then she shook her head. She could do this. She would do it.

Fighting the wave of desire washing over her, Amber moved into business mode, determined to remain detached as she washed Jordan's body, ignoring his gaze as she kept her attention on her task. Fully focused, no nurse could have done a better job, and when she was done she made quick work of her own ablutions, batting his hand away when he attempted to help. Determined not to be deterred by any distraction, she kept going until she'd scrubbed herself clean. Only then did she shut off the shower and take his hand.

She tugged at it, making him follow as she grabbed a towel from the rack and walked into the bedroom. She threw it at him and when he caught it she lifted her arms, swallowing her shyness, fixing him with a bold glare. "Get to work," she ordered.

She could tell he knew exactly what she meant. Good boy that he was, he immediately moved forward to rub the terry cloth towel over her body, his movements brisk then slowing to seductive strokes that made her slap his hand away.

She glared at him. "Get yourself dry," she ordered, "then go lie on the bed."

He lifted his brows but he did not object. Like he was eager to get going, he made quick work of the task then went over to the bed where he lay down, his body deliciously bare, his gaze disarmingly bold.

Little did he know what she had in store. If he did, he might not be so eager.

As he lay there on the bed, Amber walked over to pull her secret weapon from her travel bag. She glanced over her shoulder. "Close your eyes," she commanded.

As soon as he complied, she went over and climbed onto the bed beside the supine man. Taking advantage of his temporary lack of sight, she grasped his wrist and pushed it up toward the bedpost. When he made as if to resist, she slapped him. "Be still."

Swiftly, her sash in hand, she secured Jordan's wrist to the bedpost. Quickly, she reached across his body to secure the other.

Curiosity must have gotten the better of him because she caught him stealing a peek at her. Now it was her turn to smirk. "If you won't ravish me," she said softly, a smile slipping onto her lips, "then I'll ravish you."

Jordan did not seem the least bit perturbed by her threat. On the contrary, he defied her, refusing to keep his eyes closed, gazing at her with eyes bold as brass.

His brazen stare making her want to take him down a notch, Amber reached down to clamp his face in firm hands, making him immobile. With his hands trapped in their bonds there was nothing he could do but stare back at her.

Actually, there was one other thing he could do. He could kiss her. With her permission, of course. And this time, she was giving him exactly that.

She leaned forward to lower her lips to capture his in a searing kiss that left him breathless. But that was just the start of her planned torture.

He was straining at his bonds as he struggled to reach out and touch her but she did not yield. No, he wasn't going to touch her. She would not put that power in his hands.

Reveling in the power that was hers and hers alone, she left him to suffer as he tugged at his bonds while she slid her tongue down his body, across his pecs, over the ripples of his muscled abdomen, down toward the silky strands that snuggled softly between his thighs.

She heard his sharp intake of breath. She felt his body tense beneath her lips. She saw when his stomach muscles tightened. After all that, how could she doubt her power over him?

The sense of power making her heart swell, she leaned into him, wanting to feel him, touch him, taste him. It would be the ultimate testament to her control.

Her mind made up, knowing there was no turning back, Amber opened her mind, closed her eyes, and made a determined move toward her goal.

***

Oh, hell. Amber must have been a girl scout, she'd tied the sash so tight. Light though the fabric had seemed, it was super strong, seeming to get stronger the more he tugged at it. If only he could free his hands.

Amber's face was mere inches away, the warmth of her breath, her nearness, making him moan. God, she was such a tease. Jordan could not believe this was his unassuming assistant, now so daring, now so bold.

He was just getting used to the thought when the wicked woman did something that made his breath catch in his throat. To his astonishment...and delight...the daring girl slid her lips farther down, down, down to press them to the base of his manhood. And then she began the most sensual caress, teasing him with her tongue, making him writhe in sweet agony.

"I want to touch you," he groaned. "Release me so I can hold you."

Instead of obeying, his spontaneous dominatrix ignored him, instead focusing her attention on driving him wild. His body jerked when her lips took him captive, his breath coming in short gasps as she sent his senses soaring.

Desperation driving him mad, he bucked at his bonds, yanking hard, but the fabric only tightened more. He gazed down at the top of Amber's head, willing her to release him.

It was no use. Like she was reveling in her newfound power over him, she only heightened the torture, sliding her tongue over his skin, making him shiver at her touch.

When he thought he could bear it no longer, she drew back. It was only then that the tension that was tightening his body eased enough so that he sagged back onto the bed, his chest heaving as he sucked in air.

He was still panting as Amber crept back up his body and placed her lips close to his ear. "I have a surprise for you," she whispered, her voice silkily seductive. "Just wait right here."

If Jordan hadn't been so caught up in his helplessness he would have laughed. Tied up like he was, where else could he go? All he could do was wait.

His gaze followed Amber as she climbed off the bed and strolled seductively across the room, her hips swaying as she went. She knew exactly what she was doing to him, moving like that, her svelte body a sight that made him hard as rock.

He watched as she went over to her travel bag and pulled out yet another sash. He frowned. What did she need another sash for? To tie his legs?

Moments later, he found out. As soon as she was back by his side she leaned over, giving him a delicious view of her beautiful breasts. He licked his lips, his face moving involuntarily, tilting upward toward the tempting pink tips tilted toward him.

That was as far as he got. He had a sudden shock when a swathe of fabric fell across his face, covering his eyes, blocking his view. Next thing he knew, Amber was tying that sash behind his head, then moving away again, making him moan. "Where are you going?"

His question was greeted with a chuckle, then silence, then the feel of a hand sliding up his leg. As the hand moved north he stiffened, in anticipation of he knew not what. He could only hope. The girl had him good and trapped and he could only wait.

He soon realized that Amber meant business. As bold as you please, she grasped him and placed something cool and yielding at the tip and then she was sheathing him, making him moan yet again.

The soft groan hadn't left his lips before she was climbing onto the bed, on top of him, trapping him in so many more ways than one.

But Jordan could not complain. This entrapment, so glorious, so sensual, was more than he could have wished for. As his seductress sank down onto him he sighed his satisfaction, not able to hold it in, not able to deny his ecstasy.

His wrists still tied to the bedposts, Jordan could do nothing but give himself over to the glorious pleasure that Amber was bestowing on him.

And she was loving it. He could not see, but he could feel it in the tightening of her legs around him, the rocking of her hips, the sound of her gasps as she rode him to the brink and beyond.

"Aah." The pleasure so intense, a guttural groan was soon ripped from his lips as he hurtled over the edge, his body rigid as he reached his peak.

"Aah." Amber stiffened above him, her body clenching him and holding on, taking him in the tumultuous tide that made her dig her nails into his chest. "Oh, God," he heard her gasp and then, like her bones had liquefied, she sagged till she was lying against his chest.

As Amber melted into him, Jordan was melting too, powerless against the force of their passion, swept away in the sensuous swirl of her seduction.

It took a moment, a long moment, for them to recover. Amber was the first to make a move. He felt her shift and slowly, almost gingerly, he slid off her and settled her onto the bed beside him then cradled her head against his chest.

It was a move that made the emotions of the moment well up inside him. Filled with a tenderness that threatened to overwhelm him, he whispered the words that he hoped would win her over so she would do his bidding. "Let me loose, Amber. Let me see you. Let me hold you."

This time, his plea did not fall on deaf ears. As soon as the words left his lips he felt her reach up to release the knot behind his head. As the sash fell away he blinked, happy to see the flushed face of his captor. To his surprise, she made quick work of the knots at his wrists, freeing him at last.

Finally free, he flexed his stiff muscles then reached down to gather the now grinning girl into his arms.

"You've been a naughty one," he reprimanded as she curled against him, but his tone was too tender for her to take him seriously.

He couldn't blame her. The depth of his emotion must have been oh, so obvious. He did not doubt that she could hear it in the beat of his heart and feel it in the strength of his embrace.

It must have made her satisfied that she'd conquered him, not only in bed, but also in heart and soul.

She would be satisfied, yes. But he, on the other hand, was scared as hell.

# CHAPTER SEVEN

"Oh, no, you didn't."

"Oh, yes, I did."

When Amber heard Sasha's sharp intake of breath, she laughed. "A girl's got to break out of her shell sometime. You were the one who taught me that."

"I know. But I didn't exactly mean for you to go jump the guy."

"That's not what I did. I only-"

"No, you did worse. You practically forced yourself on the man. You had him tied up, Amber."

Amber grimaced. "You make it sound so slimy. It wasn't like that at all. He enjoyed being dominated-" A sound outside the bedroom door made her cut her sentence short. "Anyway, Sash, I've got to go. I'll call you when I get back tonight, okay?"

"You'd better." Sasha's growl ended on a chuckle "If you get up to any more antics, I want a full account."

"Okay, okay. Got to go." Amber tapped the phone and cut off the call just as Jordan entered the room.

Dressed in navy blue suit and wine-colored tie, he looked seriously handsome. Just the sight of him brought the memories rushing back. It made her mouth go dry.

He gave her a grave look. "Ready to go?"

Amber nodded, but inside she was frowning. Jordan did not seem to be his usual self. He wasn't even looking at her. What the heck was wrong with him?

The journey to the office was a quiet one and this time it wasn't Amber's fault. Every time she tried starting a conversation with Jordan he killed it quick, answering her in monosyllables, which was far from encouraging.

She was surprised when she got to the office and this time she was invited into the business meeting. Then it hit her – in having her attend the business meeting, Jordan Masters was sending her a message, a subtle one that his uncle would not pick up on, but a message he knew she would get, loud and clear. At the end of it all, when they were far from the view of Jordan's uncle, she was nothing but an employee. She could play pretend wife all she wanted. That would change nothing.

But she already knew that. So what had changed? Had it been her behavior the night before? Amber could barely meet Jordan's gaze, she was so ashamed. After that show she'd put on, what must he think of her?

Apparently, not much. That must be the reason he was acting so aloof, setting his boundaries, giving her unmistakable reminders that she was there for one reason and one reason only - to follow orders.

The thought dampening her mood, Amber spent most of the meeting avoiding Jordan's eyes. His uncle must have noticed her reticence because he paused in the middle of a sentence to regard her with a look of concern.

"Are you well, my niece?" he asked. "You are very quiet."

Not wanting to raise any suspicion, Amber gave a quick nod and a forced smile. "I'm fine, thank you. I'm just focused on listening and learning all that I can, from both of you."

He seemed to buy the story because he also nodded. "You are a very wise woman," he said gravely and then he turned to Jordan. "You have much to be thankful for."

Amber did not miss Jordan's slight glance her way nor the sardonic twist of his lips. His uncle might be impressed with her, but Jordan certainly wasn't.

It was just too much. She had to get away, out of the meeting, as far away from Jordan as she could. She could not bear his disdain a minute longer.

She reached for her glass of water and gulped down a mouthful. Then, feigning a headache, she put her hand to her forehead.

"I'm sorry," she said, then cleared her throat. "I'm sorry. Could you excuse me? I feel like...I'm coming down with something."

Sheikh Ali's brows shut up. "You are ill?"

Her gaze downcast, she shook her head. "It's nothing. Just a slight headache, that's all." Still avoiding Jordan's eyes, she turned her gaze toward the older man. "Will you excuse me for a minute?"

Quickly, he nodded then he stood up to help her from her chair. "Please, take all the time you need. I will have Riyanne take you to the lounge so you can rest." He was picking up his cell phone as he spoke.

It was not lost on Amber that Jordan had not jumped to her aid. He'd turned toward her, a frown on his face, but when his uncle had given her his arm to lean on, he'd sunk back down into his seat, his gaze glued to her. But he never said a word.

It must have taken about two minutes for Riyanne to arrive but to Amber it seemed like two hours. She wanted so badly to get away. As soon as she saw the girl, she stepped forward to take her hand.

As they left the conference room, a quick glance behind told Amber all she needed to know. The frown that still creased Jordan's brow told her he was none too pleased. Well, he could just stew. At this point, she didn't give a damn.

On the way to the lounge, Riyanne squeezed her hand. "You are ill? I am so sorry."

Feeling a twinge of guilt, Amber shook her head. "No. I'm fine. I just needed to get away."

In the elevator, her friend turned to her. "You were not enjoying the meeting?"

Amber drew in a shallow breath. "It's not that. I just wanted to get away from Jordan."

Riyanne gave her a look that was almost one of pity. "Your plan. It did not work?"

Amber gave her a rueful smile. "Just the opposite. It backfired." She gave a shrug of resignation. "It looks like he's not into the 'liberated woman' type. Oh, well."

The elevator door opened right at that moment and she stepped out. Her heart trembling with shame, she walked quickly, not glancing Riyanne's way, not wanting to see the look in the girl's eyes.

But it seemed Riyanne was having none of that. She sped up and caught Amber by the arm. "Do not be ashamed that you expressed yourself," she said fiercely. "Never be ashamed. It is a sorry man who cannot appreciate it when a woman lays her soul bare before him." Then, as they entered the lounge, the girl smiled. "There is something I will share with you," she said. "Something that will cheer you up."

Amber gave her a wan smile. "I'm all ears."

It turned out that Riyanne's story didn't cheer her up as much as it fired her determination to take control of her situation. What her friend was telling her intrigued her. No matter that she was brought up and still lived in a conservative society, Riyanne refused to be restricted in her desires. As far as she was concerned, in a relationship with the man of her dreams, behind the bedroom door she was going to explore her deepest desires.

And what she wanted was bondage.

Amber blinked. "Excuse me?"

Riyanne's look was bold and unapologetic. "Yes, that is what I said. Bondage. It is a fantasy of mine, one I would like to explore with the right man." She winked at Amber, her lips curling in sly smile. "I have the perfect man for the job."

Amber's brows shut up. "You do?"

Riyanne nodded. "I do. His name is Sheikh Khyle Mann. He does not know it yet, but he is the man I have chosen to be my husband."

"What? Is that how it works?"

The girl laughed. "Not usually, but that is how it will work for me."

Amber frowned. "How do you plan to make that happen?"

"The art of seduction, my friend. The art of seduction."

Amber folded her arms across her chest. "Explain."

Riyanne's smile widened. "I know men think they're in charge but they're really not. A woman who knows what she's doing can get anything she wants."

"And you know what you're doing."

"Of course, I do. I have a plan. By the time I am done with Khyle Mann, he will be eating out of my hands."

Amber cocked her eyebrows at her. "I find that hard to believe."

Riyanne set her mouth in a pout. "Why do you doubt me? Did I not share with you my secret weapon?"

"What secret weapon?"

"Were you not listening?" She gave a sigh of exasperation. "My weapon will be bondage."

Amber could only shake her head in disbelief. "Bondage? That's your plan?"

Riyanne was nodding eagerly. "It is. I have done much reading on it. I learned that it is a...serious turn-on for many men. I am willing and ready to try it."

Amber's lips curled in a sardonic smile. "Well, good luck with that."

"Do not laugh at me." Riyanne's eyes flashed. "You should try it with your husband. Domination did not work. Maybe you should approach things from a different angle. Try being submissive. Maybe that is what will..." she frowned like she was searching for the word, "...turn him on."

Amber grimaced, still doubtful. "I guess I could try."

Riyanne nodded. "I hope you will."

That did it for Amber. She was no wimp. Her friend was looking at her like she was wishing for an answer in the affirmative. That was exactly what she would give her.

"You don't have to hope," she said, her lips tightening in determination. "It is exactly what I will do."

Riyanne's face brightened. "And I will do the same." When Amber raised her eyebrows the girl continued. "I will be brave and make the first move toward the man of my dreams. I will seek a meeting with him." To Amber's surprise the girl reached for her phone.

"You're calling him?" she asked with a gasp. "Now?"

Riyanne smiled. "Please give me some credit. I would not be so bold." She shook her head. "No, I am calling my father. I will ask him to arrange everything." Then her smile dissolved into a chuckle. "As you would say in your country, we girls rock."

That, Amber could not deny. Both she and Riyanne would be making some bold moves but, scared though she was, she would not back out.

How could she, when it was her love that was on the line?

***

Amber hated him. Jordan could tell. The way she'd been glaring at him all morning, her eyes flashing fire, there was no doubt in his mind that his week-long wife was regretting that she'd ever agreed to the scheme to deceive his uncle. He'd thought it would have been a sweet arrangement but it was working out to be just the opposite. It looked like Amber could not get away from him fast enough.

And it was all his fault.

He'd gotten cold feet, pulling back when he should have been pushing for all he could get, maybe even as far as pushing for a commitment. Or was that wishful thinking?

"You are worried about your wife?"

His adopted uncle's words pulling him back to the present, Jordan tightened his lips then turned toward the older man. "Forgive me. You are right. I am concerned about Amber. I hope she is fine." Knowing it was the perfect excuse for his distraction, he grabbed onto it.

"You would like to go to her?" His uncle's frown was evidence of his concern.

Jordan shook his head. "No, I think I am overreacting." Then he smiled, trying to reassure Kahlil. "I know she is in good hands."

After that, Jordan did his best to clear his concerns from his mind so he could focus on the business at hand. As distracted as he was, it ended up being a long day indeed, and when it was finally time to wrap up he had to suppress a sigh of relief.

The journey back to the hotel was as quiet as the one that morning but by the time they arrived Jordan could sense that something had changed. He couldn't quite put his finger on it but, silent though she was, Amber exuded an air of quiet anticipation that he could not read. She seemed satisfied about something, some secret that was all her own. She probably would not tell him if he asked. He didn't bother to try.

Even after dinner that evening he was still trying to figure her out. Her air of quiet confidence was beginning to get to him. After the rough start they'd had that morning, what was she seeming so pleased about?

It took another couple of hours before he finally found out. After they'd showered, Amber had retired to the bedroom, leaving him alone in the living room. He'd given up on TV, finding that he wasn't in the mood for much excitement. Amber's mellow mood must have rubbed off on him because he just lay there on the sofa, eyes closed, his thoughts in turmoil.

If only he could interpret Amber's mysterious shift in mood. As he lay there, his thoughts floating back to the exciting events of the night before, he could feel his body growing taut, his breath growing shallow. God, he wanted that girl, his Amber, his beautiful pretend bride. He was growing hard just thinking about it.

And then he made a decision he hoped he would not regret. He wanted Amber too badly to just lay there like a log and not to make a move. If anything was going to happen this night, he would have to make that move, come what may.

That settled, Jordan drew in a deep breath and opened his eyes. He was swinging his legs off the sofa when what he saw made his jaw drop.

Amber, more beautiful than he'd ever seen her before, was standing in the doorway, gazing across at him.

And, to his happy astonishment, she was totally and deliciously nude.

# CHAPTER EIGHT

Oh, Lord. She'd done it now.

Amber was standing at the door, striking the most seductive pose she could muster, and Jordan was just sitting there, staring back at her, his jaw slack. Like she'd anticipated, she'd shocked him out of his wits but, contrary to her expectations, he hadn't made a move to come to her.

Here she was, all decked out in fancy footwear, sandals with heels so high she felt she would topple over, her only garment a near transparent sash she'd draped across her shoulders and over her breasts. The ends of the soft pink sash fell daintily in front, affording her a hint of modesty as it hid her most intimate element from view.

She saw when he swallowed and then he was sitting forward on the sofa, his gaze glued to her. He was staring at her so intently that she felt the pink shadow of shame creep up her body, moving up to stain her cheeks in a blush of pure embarrassment.

And still, he said not a word.

Realizing that it was in her hands, Amber swallowed, summoning the courage to follow through on her carefully made plan of seduction.

Do the opposite, Riyanne had said. Well, tonight Amber the Bully was gone. In her place Jordan was going to find the most submissive seductress he could ever want.

Her mind made up, Amber stepped out of her sandals and made her way to the sofa where Jordan sat. Before he could say a word she dropped to her knees before him.

"How may I serve you, my liege?"

"Huh?" Looking confused as heck Jordan frowned, his head tilting as he gazed down at her. If she weren't so nervous, it would be funny, seeing him so bewildered he was without words. Without coherent ones, anyway.

She decided to press her advantage. She might as well set the stage for her seduction - now, while his mind was muddled. Before he could recover, she lowered her lips and pressed them to the top of his bare foot and when he sucked in his breath she slid them up to sweetly seduce his ankle with yet another kiss.

She was surprised when she felt a gentle hand at her head, his fingers sliding through her hair as he cradled her crown with his palm. "What are you doing to me?" he groaned. "Do you have any idea what you're doing?"

Amber only smiled, his words emboldening her, making her want to make him melt under her caress. It was working, this submissive role she'd chosen, and she could not be happier. She knew exactly what she was doing. She was showing him the other side of her, the side that would free him to fulfill his naturally dominant role.

Sliding her hands up the sides of his legs she rose up until, her palms placed on top of his lap, her face tilted up toward him, she was gazing up to see the bemused expression on his face. "I am yours," she said softly, seductively. "I am here to please you. Please take me." Instead of the frown lifting from his face, it deepened. "Do you know what you're saying?" His hand shifted to cup her chin.

She smiled. "I know exactly what I'm doing," she assured him. "It gives me pleasure to be able to serve you." When he still looked hesitant, she pressed on. "I want to do this, Jordan. I really do."

Like she'd finally convinced him, he nodded. "Very well." The words were said in a serious tone but the naughty gleam in his eyes told her he was game.

And, as far as she was concerned, she was ready.

But what Jordan did next was totally unexpected. In a flash he was up, taking her with him, and before she knew what was happening he had her over his shoulder and he was he was striding toward the bedroom.

Glad that he was getting into the spirit of the game, Amber laughed out loud even as she was clinging to the back of his shirt, her head hanging down, her hair falling in a cascade down his back.

"You want to be dominated?" he growled. "You've got it."

Seconds later, Amber found herself falling onto her back on top of the bed, arms and legs splayed as she landed among the pillows. Before she could recover, Jordan was on the bed beside her, his lips sliding over the expanse of exposed skin at her midriff. God that felt delicious.

"Is this what you wanted," he whispered, "to be ravished? To be dominated by your master?"

"Yes." It was a breathless gasp that spoke to the depth of her desire. "Yes, sir, please take me. I am yours."

Like it was his license to heighten the heat, he brushed her sash aside to reveal a puckered nipple and without warning he lowered his lips to capture the burgeoning bud in the sweetest caress, a kiss so sweet that it sent tingles rippling up her spine.

"Oh, yes," she sighed. "Please don't stop."

But, to her chagrin, despite her plea, stop he did. Eyes gleaming in the shadows of the bedroom suite, Jordan's brows fell as he glared down at her. "You dare tell your master what to do?" The slight smile on his lips made a lie of his reprimand.

Amber could not have been more pleased. Jordan was game, playing along with her spoken desire for domination, and she was loving it.

His next move took her totally by surprise. Swiping the same sash that was her so slight covering, he captured her wrists in one big hand as he wrapped the silky fabric around and around, trapping her hands in front of her.

"Now," he said, his voice a soft growl, "it's your turn to be the prisoner. My captive."

The words, so softly spoken, but so sternly, shook her body with shivers of anticipation. It was like a dream come true, having him play this risqué game with her. It could only mean that the cool iceberg that had traveled in the limousine with her had melted into a hot-blooded man who was ready to ravish her oh, so willing, person.

Like he was ready for action, Jordan pressed Amber back into the pillows and then he was shucking off shirt and slacks, everything right down to his shorts, till he stood there nude and proud, the sight of him making her mouth go dry.

He must have seen when her body tightened because, with a slow smile, he slipped onto the bed beside her and slowly slid his palm over her skin. "Relax, my sweet," he whispered. "Just relax and enjoy."

Thus began the torture, the sweetest sensation she had ever experienced. When Jordan dipped his head and sucked her throbbing bud into his mouth she felt like she would die from the ecstasy but when his hand slid down to cup her mound, to tantalize that tender tumescence till it throbbed beneath his caress, she knew it would not be much longer before she would topple over the edge. She lifted her bound hands, wanting to hold him there, close to her heart, but to her disappointment he moved away, leaving her bereft.

But not for long.

Within seconds, Jordan was back and with a vengeance, sliding his tongue along the curves of her breasts, skirting the smooth slope of her shoulders and up the soft skin at her neck until he had captured her lips with his own. There, he paused to plunder and pillage until he had her gasping. Still, he did not let up. It was when she reached up to dig desperate fingers into his chest that he drew back.

When he gazed down at her, his eyes were dark with the intensity of his passion. "The best way you can serve me," he said gruffly, "is by obeying my every command. Will you do that?"

Amber had no idea what Jordan had in mind and she didn't care. She nodded. "Yes, sir" she whispered. "I will obey."

His next move made her wonder if, in agreeing, she'd made a mistake. In one swift move he was off the bed but then he was back, a tie in his hand, and the next thing she knew he'd covered her eyes and was securing that sash at the back of her head. She'd never felt so vulnerable in her life.

"What are you doing?" she asked, her voice an uncertain gasp as she struggled to adjust to her new state that was totally devoid of sight.

He chuckled, and in the forced darkness, his voice almost sounded ominous. "What I should have done before," he said, his voice suspiciously silky. "Teach you what it means to yield to the ministrations of your master."

Not knowing what he meant, Amber gulped, her heart pounding as she awaited his pleasure. How did he expect her to serve him? What did he mean when he said she should yield? Did he really mean to make love to her like this, bound and blind as she was?

The thoughts were still swirling around in her head, uncertainty making her heart pound in her chest, when his palm cupping her breasts made her forget it all, everything except the feel of his fingers warming her skin, the teasing of his thumb as it toyed with her nipple.

"Oh, God," she groaned. "Please stop torturing me. Let me see you. Let me touch you. Please."

His response was a terse command. "You are to obey," he said sternly, "without question. Now you must relax and let me do as I wish."

Amber gulped again but she did not object. "Yes, master," she whispered, "whatever you wish." She was in his hands, totally powerless, and for some strange reason it felt so freeing. She'd given herself over to the man she loved, first in body and now in mind.

When she felt Jordan shift over her body she sighed, expecting him to settle himself against her so that she could please him the best way she knew how. But it did not happen.

Instead of pausing in the expected position, Jordan kept going down, down until he'd settled between the softness of her thighs. There, he commenced a caress so intimate that he made her jerk in surprise and then he had her writhing from the sheer pleasure of it all.

Within seconds he had her crying out and even then he did not stop. The faster her pants the sweeter his strokes, until she was jerking against him in the throes of a passion that threatened to tear her apart.

At least, that was what it felt like - the thunderous pounding of her heart, the gasping for air, the sweet spasms that were sweeping through her body. "Jordan. Oh, please, Jordan." Her inane babble was testament to her addled state, swept up in a swirl of sensation intensified by her captive state.

With no sense of sight, with all other senses heightened, his tender touch was such stimulation to her sensitive skin that the lightest of strokes soon sent her tumbling over the edge. The ecstasy of her orgasm rippling through her, she reached down to dig her fingers into his hair.

It was long moments before Amber returned to the real world, her panting slowing as she floated down from the cluster of clouds on which she'd landed in her flight of ecstasy.

She was still sliding back to solid ground when she felt firm fingers loosening the bonds at her wrists then gently lifting her head to loosen the strip of fabric that had been tied there. As the sash slipped from her face, she blinked.

It took a moment for her eyes to focus and when they did, it was to find Jordan gazing back at her. Immediately, the heat began to rise up her body, all the way up until it was suffusing her face.

Her embarrassment must have been obvious because he gave her a gentle smile then he was moving up the bed to lay down beside her.

Still flushed and flustered, Amber tucked her face against the warm strength of his shoulder. Jordan had taken her to the brink and beyond. He'd been the one doing the serving. Now it was her turn.

Wanting to share the pleasure, she slid her hand along his arm then shifted till she was moving down the length of him.

Jordan reached out to palm her shoulder, stilling her movement. "Where are you going?" he asked.

She tucked her face against him again, this time pressing against the firmness of his stomach. "I'm going to please you," she said, her voice muffled. "It is my turn to serve you."

What he did next was not what she expected. Instead of letting her continue on her way, he placed strong hands beneath her arms and pulled her up till she was lying on top of him, her cheek pressed against his chest.

Before she could move...not that she wanted to...he was wrapping his arms around her, his embrace so warm and so gentle, that it brought an unexpected tear to her eye.

His next words made things even worse, making her have to fight to hold in the tears. "Just stay here with me," he said softly. "You've served me well enough. Now just let me hold you." Those words, so softly spoken, were like a salve to her soul. She'd been suffering for so long, wanting this man, her boss, to notice her, wanting him to fall in the same way she'd fallen so long ago. She wanted him to love her.

And now he'd spoken those words. But what did they mean? Could it be, he was beginning to feel for her the same way she felt about him?

It was a question she was scared to ask. For the moment, she would just accept what he had to give.

That decided, Amber breathed a sigh of satisfaction as she relaxed into the embrace of the man she'd let dominate, not just her body, but also her heart.

# CHAPTER NINE

Amber was on cloud nine. Everybody could see it, even Riyanne.

"Amber, are you with me?" For the third time that morning her friend had to pull her back to the present, forcing her to reel in her roaming thoughts and pay attention.

But how could she, when right then she was the happiest girl in the world?

"You're not feeling ill again, are you?" Riyanne was staring at her, concern etched on her face.

Amber chuckled. "No, not at all. Just the opposite. I never felt so good in my life."

That made the other girl frown. "What do you mean? Did something happen?"

Amber nodded, unable to suppress her joy. "Something very good happened. I think...I think Jordan finally understands me."

Riyanne looked curious. "He does? He said so?"

Amber shrugged. "Well, not exactly. But sometimes actions speak louder than words."

Riyanne blinked. "Actions. What did he do?"

Amber only smiled and shook her head. Elated though she was, there were some things she would rather keep to herself. She heaved a satisfied sigh. "Let's just say, things are looking pretty positive for Jordan and me."

"But things were already good for you and your husband, were they not?" There was a slight look of confusion on in Riyanne's eyes.

That was when Amber realized she'd almost messed up. Jordan was already her husband, as far as Riyanne knew. She'd forgotten about that. Time for damage control. "Good," she agreed, "but now things are even better."

Wanting to move to safer ground, she quickly changed the subject and soon she and Riyanne were busy planning how her newfound friend could visit her back in California someday soon.

Amber's good mood lasted all day but then something happened that made her wonder if something was wrong. Jordan was unusually quiet on the way back to the hotel but what was more disconcerting was the way he responded when she made what she thought was an innocent joke.

"Cat got your tongue?" she quipped.

His response was sharp. "It might have been good if you'd let the cat get yours."

Amber frowned. What the heck was that supposed to mean? She never got the chance to demand an explanation because, right at that moment, they pulled up in front of the hotel. Swallowing her annoyance, she was silent as she took the hand he offered and stepped out of the car.

As soon as they'd stepped into the hotel suite and Jordan closed the door behind them, Amber whirled around to glare at him. "What was that, about letting the cat get my tongue? What are you insinuating?"

Instead of backing off, Jordan straightened and folded his arms across his chest. "I'm not insinuating anything. I'm saying this, loud and clear. You talk too darned much."

Shocked at the rudeness of his response, she sucked in her breath. "You take that back, Jordan Masters."

"I will not. It's clear to me now, I should never have trusted you to Riyanne's care. My incorrigible cousin is up to her old tricks and she's taken you along for the ride."

Amber tilted her head. "Meaning what?"

"Riyanne told Khalil about this crazy scheme she cooked up, to get a chance to rendezvous with Sheikh Mann. In the conversation with her father it slipped out that she had some kinky plan in mind. Something to do with bondage." His brows fell and the look he gave her was dark with suspicion. "That sounds familiar. Did you put Riyanne up to this? Did you tell her about us?"

Amber's heart clenched tight in her chest. "Is that what you think?"

"What do you expect me to think? Is it a coincidence that what she said was a perfect match for how you've been behaving these last couple of nights?" When she didn't respond right away, he gave a snort. "Can't deny it, can you? You and Riyanne have been cooking up crazy seduction schemes and I was the guinea pig. You took me for a fool, dammit." His lips twisting in obvious disgust, he turned away from Amber and stomped back toward the door. There, he paused to glare back at her. "It's a good thing we're leaving tomorrow. For me, this husband-wife farce can't end fast enough." With that, he marched out the door, closing it sharply behind him.

In shock, Amber could not move. For several seconds she just stood there, staring at the door. What had just happened? How in the world had everything suddenly gone wrong?

When it finally sank in, that she'd made a horrible mistake, that because of it she would lose Jordan forever, she stumbled toward the door.

But what was the use? Jordan was already gone. And on top of that, what could she say to make things right?

Devastated, Amber sagged against the solid surface of the door then, hopelessness overwhelming her, she slid down till she slumped to the ground, wishing it would open up and swallow her whole.

***

Darned women.

Still mumbling to himself, Jordan lifted the glass of whisky to his lips and gulped the fiery brew. It made him gasp, the caustic liquid lighting up his insides, but he didn't care. Right then he needed something to take his mind off his misery.

Amber Lee had used a wicked scheme to play him for a fool, and she'd taken his cousin along with her. Or was it the other way around? Right then, his mind was so muddled, he couldn't even think straight. One thing he knew, though, was that he would never forgive Amber for playing him like that.

His mind in a morose muddle, Jordan lifted the glass and took another sip before glancing around the hotel bar. It was early yet and the place was almost deserted, which was probably a good thing. He was in no mood to be mixing and mingling with anyone, least of all a happy, chattering crowd.

He was sitting there, shoulders slumped, wallowing in self-pity, when a sharp voice jerked him out of his depressed reverie.

"That's your third," the voice said. "It's kind of early for this, isn't it? Want to take a break?"

He looked up to see a blond woman, probably close to sixty, smiling at him.

"Drowning your sorrows?" she asked, seeming unfazed by his glare.

He shrugged, in no mood for conversation. Maybe his lack of response would rid him of her.

It didn't.

Instead of disappearing, the woman came closer, her hands occupied with the glass she was wiping. "Clearly, you've got lots on your mind, but indulge me for a minute. I've seen and heard it all, so I'll give you a word of advice, if you don't mind." That was a joke. She looked like she had advice and she was going to give it, whether he minded or not. "Whatever is bothering you, if it's a decision you've got to make, at the back of your mind always think of the impact your immediate decision will have on your life ten years from now. Don't shoot from the hip in the heat of the moment. Take a minute. Pause and ponder where you want to be ten years from today. That will help you make the best decision...for you."

Slowly, Jordan lowered the glass and laid it on the counter. He swiveled on the barstool till he was staring directly at the woman. He frowned. "Are you some kind of psychic?" The woman's advice made so much sense, it was eerie.

She laughed. "Maybe I am. After almost forty years as a barmaid, I might as well be one."

It was a thoughtful Jordan who made his way to the elevator minutes later. He'd been a fool, overreacting like he had, to Amber's unorthodox attempt at seduction. So what if it had been a plan cooked up while in the company of his wayward cousin? It didn't hurt anything except his too fragile ego.

Like the woman said, ten years from now, what would matter more? That he'd been manipulated by a diminutive girl, or that he'd walked away from the woman who'd had him fighting to suppress his love all this time?

Well, not anymore. It was time for him to man up and make his feelings known. There was no way he was going to miss this moment, not when so much...his love...was at stake.

When he got to the door, he drew in a deep breath then put his hand on the knob. When he opened and stepped in, he was ready.

Time to apologize.

# CHAPTER TEN

The nerve of the man. To reprimand her for expressing her desire in a way that was slightly out of the norm? How dare he?

Well, she was not going to take that sitting down. She would not apologize for letting her feelings be known. If the feeling was not mutual, then so be it. All he had to do was say so. But to judge her for being upfront with her feelings? Hmmph.

When Jordan had stormed out of the suite she'd almost given in to despair but, thank goodness, she'd caught herself. Once she had, her despair had morphed into anger, righteous anger that made her plant herself by the door, arms crossed, ready to tackle the man who had made her mad.

She didn't have to wait long. A little over thirty minutes from the time he marched out, the door opened and there, in the entrance, stood her boss.

She did not even wait for him to close the door behind him. Before he could say a word, she launched her attack. "Jordan Masters, you treated me like dirt just now and I'm not going to stand for it. I placed my heart on a platter and offered it to you, not once but twice, and all you could do was throw it back in my face? You could at least have had the decency to wait until we got back to California. That way I could have simply walked away and not be stuck with you for the next twenty-four hours." She tossed her head in annoyance, and when her hair fell across her forehead she released her crossed arms to put a hand up to brush the floating strands from her face. "From the first time I came to you, you should have told me you weren't interested. You didn't have to wait till I threw myself at you a second time and then-"

"Are you done?" Like he was tired of her tirade, Jordan cut in, his face dark like a thundercloud.

"Yes, I'm done," she retorted. "There's nothing more to say. I won't even waste my time." That said, she whirled away and began to stalk off toward the bedroom.

She didn't get far. She was halfway there when she was surprised by a sharp command.

"Stop right there."

It was such a shock that she obeyed. Too confused to be angry, she turned. "What did you say?"

His face set like a rain cloud, his response was a rough growl. "Is this the way you speak to your master? Come back here."

Amber's jaw went slack, her eyes widening as she stared back at him. What was he saying? How could he want to play the game at a time like this?

Heart thumping, thrown totally off-balance, she took a step toward him, then paused.

Apparently, her hesitation did not please him. His frown deepening, he spoke again. "I said, come here."

Deciding to demonstrate her defiance by doing just as he ordered, she took the steps that placed her no more than a foot away. She was there, just like he'd commanded. Now what was he going to do about it? What could he do? He wasn't going to touch her without permission, she knew that much.

She balled her fingers into fists and jammed them on her hips as she glared up at him. "What do you want?"

"Kiss me."

The order caught her off guard. "What?"

"You heard me. Are you going to be a good submissive and obey, or do you want me to ravish you right here?"

Her lips curled in a defiant smile. "I dare you."

The words were hardly out of her mouth before Jordan was pulling her into his arms.

She hadn't expected that. Pulled up till she was on tiptoe, there was not much she could do to resist. Expecting certain punishment, she steeled herself for a forceful fusion.

What happened next was quite the opposite.

Jordan seduced her lips with a kiss so sweet that all Amber could do was melt into his arms. Defiant though she'd planned to be, she was succumbing to the sweetness of his embrace and there was nothing she could do to help it. When he finally drew away, she was panting.

As she clung to Jordan, her eyes still cloudy as she gazed up at him, his arm wrapped around her tightened.

To her surprise, for a moment he looked like was searching for words. When he finally spoke, his voice was solemn. "Will you forgive me?" he asked. "You offered me what I'd been praying for, all this time but I, like a fool, refused what you were giving." He released her, but only so he could slide his palms up her arms and place her just far enough where he could look directly into her eyes. "Amber, would you consider having a fool for a husband?"

Her heart leaping to her throat, Amber gasped. "What are you saying?"

"I'm saying," his voice fell lower still, "Amber, will you be my wife? Not just a pretend wife, but my wife...for real."

Her hands rose involuntarily, and then she was clinging to his shirt. "Are you serious?"

His lips curled in a sardonic smile. "Does it look like I'm joking?"

It was all Amber needed to hear. "Then my answer is yes, Jordan. I will be your real wife. Gladly."

"My love." His voice was thick with emotion. "You've made me the happiest man in the world."

Her response was a hiccup. "And I'm the happiest woman."

He cocked his head to one side as he gazed down at her. "You're sure? You're not just saying that?"

She fixed him with a scorching glare. "Do you need me to drag you off to the bedroom and tie you up to prove it?"

The tension in his lips relaxed into a satisfied smile. "No, my love. I believe you." Then a teasing twinkle gleamed in his eyes. "We've got plenty of time for you to dominate me. I look forward to it."

Happily, she smiled right back. "So do I."

Poor Jordan. He didn't know what he'd signed up for.

Let the games begin.

## Thank you for reading!
I hope you enjoyed 'A is for Arrangement'.
If so, your review would be greatly appreciated.


Please look out for the next in the series:

# B is for Bondage

Growing up in the Middle East, Riyanne is quite familiar with the culture of the harem. She's always been fascinated with the lifestyle...and just a little bit scared.

When Sheikh Khyle Mann agrees to take her under his wing and tutor her in the ways of his world, she is overwhelmed.

Does she have the courage to give in to her wildest fantasy...of being the bonded bride of a powerful man?

by Eden Adams
Leading the Way in Diversity

Curious about Sasha's story? Check it out:

# THE BILLIONAIRE'S BOLD BET

# JUDY ANGELO

An Erotic Romance Adventure

*"I can have any woman I want."*

Corporate magnate Dante Perakis is uber-confident in his ability to charm any woman on the planet. He is so confident, in fact, that he takes on the bet thrown out by his long-time friend, Raffaello Palazzo, that within only two weeks he will get powerhouse tycoon, Sasha Force, to fall for him. The only problem is, he can't reveal his true identity. He must charm this heiress to the Force Factor multi-million dollar empire while pretending to be a working class man. Will his manly charms be enough?

Sasha Force doesn't believe in mixing and mingling with 'the help' but Dante Perakis is like no other working class man she has ever met. He demonstrates a level of knowledge of the business world that has her jaw dropping in pleasant surprise and admiration. This man is way too smart to be a blue collar worker, and it doesn't hurt that he's smooth, suave and super sexy, too. Against her better judgment she finds herself falling for him. But then she finds that, behind his charming exterior, he's as deceitful as they come. Sexy or not, she wants him gone.

Even though he's messed up, can Dante convince Sasha that he's the man for her? In the end, will love save the day?

# CHAPTER ONE

"I can have any woman I want. There isn't even a question about that." Dante Perakis leaned back in his chair and clasped his hands behind his head, a satisfied smile on his lips.

"You're so full of it, it's not even funny." Raffaello Palazzo was shaking his head as he stared across his desk at his friend. "Just because you have half of the girls in San Francisco throwing themselves at you it doesn't mean you can have any woman you want."

Dante cocked an eyebrow at him. "Wanna bet?"

Rafe folded his arms, a smirk curling his lips. "So you're up for a challenge, are you? That's good because I have the perfect woman for you."

Dante gave him a confident smile in response. "Who is it? Does that beautiful wife of yours have a sister I don't know about?"

"You should be so lucky. No, the woman in question is a friend of mine, a formidable force in the business world." He chuckled. "That's her name, by the way, and quite appropriate."

"What's her name?" Dante frowned, confused.

"Force. Sasha Force. You've heard of her, I'm sure."

He nodded. "She gave a presentation last year at the chamber of commerce meeting." He grimaced. "A looker, but she seems like a real ice queen."

Rafe laughed. "You've got that right." Then he jerked his chin toward Dante. "Just the right kind of woman to test your talent. Are you up to it?"

Dante cocked his head to one side, still doubtful. "Of all the women in California you could choose, why that one?"

"I told you, she's a friend." He shrugged. "I told her, with her ice-cold demeanor, if she doesn't start loosening up a bit she's going to scare off any man who might have any thought of approaching. One day she's going to turn sixty-five then turn around and ask, where did all the men go?" On his lips was a wry smile. "It would take a special man to break through that stony exterior. I wonder if you're that man?"

That made Dante shake his head, his lips curling in amusement. "Surely, you jest. Are you questioning my skills? There's no woman who can resist my charms, not even your formidable Sasha Force."

"All right. Sounds good. Just tell me when you can clear a good two weeks from your calendar and I'll arrange everything."

That made Dante frown. "Why would I need to clear my schedule? What am I going to do? Move in with the woman?"

Rafe chuckled. "Not yet, anyway. If I get my wish that's where this will end up eventually." He breathed a satisfied sigh. "Since you're considering the proposition, for two weeks I'll need you to stay in town. No out-of-town trips, do you understand? During those two weeks you will be on call, ready to move at the drop of a hat."

If Dante had been confused before, now he was even more so. "What the heck are you talking about?"

"You pride yourself on being such a charmer that you can have any woman at your beck and call," Rafe said. "So far you've done pretty well in the ladies' department. I'll give you that, but you've had a distinct advantage which few men have." Rafe cocked an eyebrow. "You're a billionaire."

Dante shrugged. "I am what I am."

Rafe chuckled. "Not for this project, you're not. It's way too easy for a billionaire to impress a lady so here's the bet. Sasha isn't a fan of driving so she gets chauffeured around a lot. Besides, she's always on her tablet or her laptop so she doesn't like to waste time maneuvering through traffic. For two weeks you will be her limo driver, an ordinary working class kind of guy. That's the man I want her to fall in love with. If you can get Sasha Force, corporate executive and heiress to a cosmetics empire, to fall in love with a regular kind of guy I'll give you my Ferrari. If you lose your McLaren is mine. Deal?"

As Dante stared back at Rafe, his words sinking in, his gaze narrowed. "You send a man on a mission then you deny him his most effective weapon? You're a dog. You know that, right?"

Rafe only laughed. "I'm trying to help a friend who needs a nudge from the right man. She's a hard-headed tyrant but I think there's hope for her yet. I'm hoping you'll be the one to break down those barriers she's built up over the years." He shrugged. "The bet's on the table. You can take it or leave it."

Dante got up and shoved his hands inside his pockets as he looked down at Rafe. "You know I'm the kind of man who can't walk away from a bet, especially one that involves a woman." He turned away and walked over to grab his jacket from the sofa where he'd thrown it when he'd walked into Rafe's office twenty minutes earlier. He shrugged into it then turned back to face his friend, a confident smile on his lips. "You're on," he said, his smile widening into a grin. "Get that Ferrari cleaned up and ready for me. By the time I'm done with Miss Sasha Force she'll be eating out of my hand."

Rafe didn't look worried. "I'm not sure you know the kind of lady you'll be dealing with. All I can say is, good luck. You're going to need it."

As Dante walked out of his office, his friend was still laughing. That was when a troubling thought began to prick his mind. What did Rafe know about Sasha Force that he didn't?

He shrugged and kept on walking. He knew he would soon find out.

***

Sasha Force was not amused. She'd given the maid strict instructions to have a light meal ready when she got home. She'd been home fifteen minutes already and dinner was still not on the table.

"What's your excuse this time?" she demanded, glaring at the uniformed girl who was hurrying to set the table.

"I'm sorry, ma'am," the girl stuttered. "It's only my second day here. I wasn't sure where to find the things."

Sasha gave a snort which was half disgust, half exasperation. Where did they find these people? This was the third less-than-satisfactory temp the agency had sent her in less than two weeks. Not one of them had lasted a week. Now she was on her third and she was this close to firing the girl. She glared at her. "I'm going out tonight and I'm not going to be late because of you. I'll be back in five minutes and dinner had better be on the table." She didn't bother to say, or else. That wasn't necessary. If the girl had any sense she would have gotten the message loud and clear. Head held high, she walked out of the dining room, her lips tightening as she heard the maid scurrying to comply.

Sasha Force was a ruthless businesswoman and even outside of the boardroom she was as cold as they came. As the boss, whether at the office or to her household staff, she was as firm as she was cold. She had to be. As the woman in charge she had to show her team, both men and women, that she was not someone to be trifled with. That was the only way they would take her seriously. She ran a tight ship and the only way she'd been able to do that was by being a true iron lady.

The girl was new, she would admit that, but she was also slow. For that, there was no excuse. Sasha had never been soft and she wasn't about to start now.

Five minutes later when she returned to the dining room the meal was laid out in silver bowls on the table. "Now that's more like it," she said under her breath. Out loud she said, "Thank you, Cindy. From here on let's stick to this schedule, shall we?"

When the maid nodded and backed out of the room she took her seat, not sparing the girl another thought. She was thinking about her father, the patriarch of the family, the one who'd made her the strong woman she'd become. She was grateful to him for it. She'd relied on his expertise and experience and even though she'd tried to live up to the Force legacy, even though she was running a successful company, she still felt like she had to do more. Her father expected so much of her. That was why she never eased up in her drive to make Force Factors a top cosmetic brand in the United States. She had to prove to her father and all of the family that she was worthy of the Force name.

Knowing that Amber would soon be there, Sasha ate quickly. She was always punctual, even for social matters. She had no intention of making her friend turn up and have to wait while she got ready for their night on the town. Within half an hour she'd finished eating. She was dressed and putting on the finishing touches to her make-up when the maid came to get her. "Miss Lee is here," the girl said. "I asked her to make herself comfortable in the sitting room."

Sasha nodded. "Very good. Tell her I'll be right down." As the maid turned to go she stopped her. "By the way, what's your name?" The agency had told her but, for the life of her, she could not remember the name. The fact that she'd hardly spoken to the servant did not help.

"My name is Tanya, ma'am. Tanya Parkhouse."

She nodded. "Tanya. That's easy enough to remember. Thank you, Tanya. Please be sure to make Miss Lee comfortable until I get there."

"Yes, ma'am."

Before the words were even out of the girl's mouth Sasha was turning back to the mirror. She wanted to look good tonight. She and Amber were going out on the town to catch men. She would look nothing less than sizzling hot.

When she walked into the sitting room Amber was relaxing on the sofa, sipping a glass of red wine. Her friend looked up and smiled. "That's a very nice lady you have working for you. She seemed so concerned that I should be comfortable." Then she cocked her head to one side. "What happened to that other lady? The one who had the mole on her left cheek. She was pretty nice, too."

Sasha grimaced. "I fired her. Too friendly for my liking. She was always calling me Sasha."

Amber shrugged. "So? That's your name, isn't it?"

"Not for the help, it's not. To them, I'm Miss Force or ma'am. I'm not their friend."

"Oh, Sasha, come off your high horse before you tumble off. This is twenty-first century America, not England in the Victorian era. Why do you have to be so formal?"

"That's how the servants always addressed Mother and Father when I was growing up so that's how I expect to be addressed."

Amber rolled her eyes. "There goes the girl with the chip on her shoulder. Will you get over it, already? So you were adopted into a rich family. Get over it, will you? You don't have to put on airs. Just be your darned self."

Sasha waved her off. "Stop lecturing me. Hurry up with your wine so we can get out of here."

Amber finished it in one gulp. "Well, that's it for me for tonight. No more imbibing since, as usual, I'm stuck being the designated driver." She gave Sasha a pointed look.

"Don't blame me because I'm no fan of driving. I told you I could have a limo over but did you accept the offer? Oh, no. You said you'd be happy to drive. Don't throw it on me."

Amber gave her a wry smile. "All right. You got me. I just didn't want some limo driver to cramp our style. What if we meet some nice guys and decide to stay super late at the nightclub? We would have some guy outside waiting for us, antsy because he wants to get home to his wife."

That didn't mean a thing to Sasha. She only shrugged. "He'd be getting paid, wouldn't he? Double time after eleven o'clock. A win-win situation, if you ask me."

Amber tossed her head. "Whatever. I still don't want any man outside, waiting on us."

Sasha didn't bother to answer that. All she knew was that Amber had better not complain about not being able to drink because she would have to drive them home. She'd been given a viable option which she'd turned down. Being a teetotaler tonight was totally her choice.

They got to Temple just after ten o'clock that night, after killing time watching a romantic comedy flick at Century Center. They hadn't wanted to arrive too early when the forty and fifty-year-olds were out. The after-ten crowd would be perfect. That was when the twenty to thirty-year-olds came out, the right set with men of the right age.

It was a Friday night and the dance floor was crowded, just as it always was on a holiday weekend. Labor Day would be in two days and many of the patrons were college and grad students trying to squeeze the last ounce of fun out of summer before they had to lose themselves in their books. Sasha wasn't interested in that set, though. She was here because this was also the watering hole for many of the city's young executives. It was that caliber of man that interested her - corporate executives or business owners, nothing less.

There were many women there without male partners, just groups of girls dancing together, so she didn't feel out of place hanging out with Amber. In fact, the DJ was doing such a great job that she soon forgot her primary reason for being there and just gave herself over to the music, bopping and bouncing to the hip hop, pop and rock rhythms, laughing out loud as Amber tried to copy her moves without much success.

She was bent over with laughter when she felt someone tap her on the shoulder. She straightened and turned to find a neatly-bearded man of medium height smiling at her. He said something but with the music pounding in her ears she couldn't hear a word. She didn't need to hear him to know what he wanted, though. He was asking her to dance.

Her movements stilled as she looked him up and down. He was wearing a department store business suit and his shoes had obviously been bought at an outlet store. The slight mismatch in the shoelaces said it all. When her gaze traveled back up his body, past his bargain store watch and faux-silk tie, she saw that his face was turning pink.

So he didn't like to be scrutinized, did he? She crinkled her nose. "No, thank you," she said, knowing quite well that he wouldn't be able to hear the words. She had no doubt that he would get the message, though. The look of disdain she gave him would be enough.

His face now fully red, the man swallowed then turned and stumbled away, bumping into the dancers who were blocking his path to escape. Seconds later he disappeared into the crowd.

Shaking her head in amusement, she turned back toward Amber, still not believing that guy. The nerve of him. Clearly, he was a nobody. And to think he would approach a woman like her. Didn't he know who she was? And even if he didn't, couldn't he see that she had way more class than pretty much all the women in the club? He must have known he would need to be a man of serious standing to even think of asking a woman like her to dance.

She was still smiling to herself when she glanced across at her friend. She did not look amused.

Before she could even say a word, Amber grabbed her by the shoulders and pulled her close so she could speak above the music, directly into her ear. "Why the heck did you do that? That was a nice man you just rejected. You hurt his feelings."

"What do I care?" Sasha retorted. "I'm not going to waste my time dancing with some low-level office worker. Can't he see that I'm no ordinary woman? I want to be approached by a man who is at my level or at least a man who knows how to dress. Did you see his bargain basement suit?" She chuckled.

Instead of laughing with her, Amber shook her head. "You're unbelievable. You may have just refused the perfect man for you. Who says he has to be rich and powerful, as long as he's genuine?" She tightened her grip on Sasha's shoulders. "At the rate you're going, you may be sixty before you find a man who is good enough, if ever."

Sasha put her hands on Amber's and pried her fingers loose, but not before making her position very clear. "That's fine by me," she grated.

"I'm only interested in a certain caliber of man, one who can be my equal in accomplishments even if not in worth. I will settle for nothing less."

As Amber drew back she slipped in a parting shot. "You just keep declaring that, my friend. Life can be ironic sometimes. The man you end up falling in love with might just be a regular kind of guy...or worse."

"Me? Fall in love with Mr. Nobody?" Sasha sneered. "That will never happen."

Slowly, Amber shook her head as she gazed back at her. "For your sake, I hope not."

Available from your favorite online retailer

A is for Arrangement
Copyright © 1664870 Ontario Ltd.
2014

# Don't miss out!

Visit the website below and you can sign up to receive emails whenever EDEN ADAMS publishes a new book. There's no charge and no obligation.

https://books2read.com/r/B-A-RLHE-PRJN

**BOOKS 2 READ**

Connecting independent readers to independent writers.

# Also by EDEN ADAMS

**FREE YOUR FANTASY Spicy Romance**
A is for Arrangement